MAX TRUEBLOOD
AND THE
JERSEY DESPERADO

Also by Teri White

TRIANGLE
BLEEDING HEARTS
TIGHTROPE

MAX TRUEBLOOD
AND THE
JERSEY DESPERADO

Teri White

CENTURY
LONDON   MELBOURNE   AUCKLAND   JOHANNESBURG

First published in Great Britain in 1988 by
Century Hutchinson Ltd
Brookmount House, 62-65 Chandos Place,
London WC2N 4NW

Century Hutchinson South Africa (Pty) Ltd
PO Box 337, Bergvlei, 2012 South Africa

Century Hutchinson Australia Pty Ltd
PO Box 496, 16-22 Church Street,
Hawthorn, Victoria 3122, Australia

Century Hutchinson New Zealand Limited
PO Box 40-086, Glenfield, Auckland 10,
New Zealand

British Library Cataloguing in Publication Data

White, Teri
    Max Trueblood and the Jersey desperado.
    I. Title
    813'.54 (F)   PS3573.H474/
    ISBN 0-7126-1958-5

Printed and bound in Great Britain by
Anchor Brendon Ltd, Tiptree, Essex

*This edition published by arrangement with
The Mysterious Press, New York*

*This book is dedicated
to my grandfather.*

*With special thanks
to those who provide
encouragement and
those who inspire me.*

MAX TRUEBLOOD
AND THE
JERSEY DESPERADO

ONE OF THE BEST OF THE BAD GUYS

one:

golden age

It was the first time in forty years that Max Trueblood had been caught without a gun when he needed one.

But who the hell did the grocery shopping with a .357 under his arm?

Even in Manhattan?

For all those years, of course, he had gone everywhere with a weapon strapped to his body—usually more than one, if truth were known. It was a habit that kept him alive. But the other side of habit, the dangerous side, was complacency. That meant getting fat and lazy and doing something stupid. Like picking out fresh artichokes unarmed, which could get a man a fatal dose of lead poisoning.

But dammit all to hell and back, he was retired now. Shouldn't that entitle a man to ease up just a little?

Apparently not.

Up until the moment when the morning went bad on him, Max had been feeling fine. He always enjoyed his weekly shopping trip around the neighborhood. This area had been his home for a very long time, for years before it became fashionable or even altogether legal for him to have been living there. When he bought his property, it was cheap and undesirable. A lot had changed in Soho since then, but he didn't mind. Mostly the march of so-called progress just amused him.

All of which was fine and good, but still no reason for stupidity.

Before things went wrong, he was crossing Broome Street when a high, squeaky voice sounded from behind, stopping him at the curb. He turned. "Morning, Buggy."

"Got a sure thing in the fifth today," the midget said. As usual, he was decked out in the manner of a Southern planter of the old school—white suit, Panama hat, cane. He waved a fat black Havana—where the hell did he get them anyway?—at Max. "Pretty little filly named Take A Chance."

Buggy's sure things were never all that sure, but they came through often enough to keep a man hoping, which, of course, was the idea. But Max was in a good mood, so he put five on the filly's nose and sent Buggy away whistling.

As Max moved on he caught a glimpse of himself reflected in a sparkling store window. Not bad for an old man, he decided. Because he still worked out semi-regularly, none of his muscle had turned to flab. Years ago someone had described him as having the build of a Sherman tank, and he thought that still applied. He was just over six feet tall and weighed within twenty-five pounds of what he had at thirty.

Admittedly, the hair on top was mostly gone and what remained was white, but maybe that just made him look distinguished. What mattered most, anyway, was that he took care of himself. Some men retired; they let themselves fall apart. Max saw them all the time, sitting in the park or riding the subways. Frayed sweaters, baggy pants, nothing looking pressed. Hell, they couldn't even be bothered to shave. Those were men who had lost their self-respect. Bums.

That would never happen to Max Trueblood.

Today he was wearing crisp white linen trousers with a knife-sharp crease, a blue pin-striped shirt, and leather sandals. In deference to this unexpected September heat wave he had donned dark glasses and his Dodger baseball cap. The hat looked a little tired because it dated from the days when the Bums still played in Brooklyn, before they moved west and became Hollywood flits.

Well, maybe that was a bit harsh, but Max still carried a grudge.

Crossing Canal Street, he walked until he reached the Vinyl Pizza. The window display had been changed since his last visit, and he paused to examine the brightly colored album covers, realizing somewhat ruefully that not one of the musical groups was familiar. Time moved on.

The small bell above the door sounded its annoyingly cheerful greeting as Max entered. Inside the store it was cool and smelled vaguely of sticky-sweet incense.

"Hiya, Max." Danni—what the hell kind of name was that for a woman, anyway?—appeared from the back room. She was smiling, as always seeming glad to see him. Maybe she treated all her customers that way. Danni wasn't what he would have called pretty, had he bothered to think about it at all, but her sturdy figure wore the jeans and T-shirt well, and her long hair was always pulled back neatly. He didn't know how old she was, probably somewhere in her thirties, but she knew music, even his kind of music. He enjoyed talking to her.

She held up the two earthenware mugs. "Coffee's ready," she said. "See, I can predict just when you'll walk through the door."

They both sat at the small wicker table. "Maybe I'm in a rut," Max said after tasting the coffee. It was instant, of course.

"No, not a rut," she protested. "You're just . . . dependable."

He grunted. It sounded like a rut to him, and he didn't like it much.

Danni took a crumpled pack of cigarettes out of a pocket

and lit one. She studied him through the cloud of gray-white smoke. "Finally got the Charlie Parker you wanted."

"Good. What about the Bud Powell?"

She shook her head. "Max, can I ask you something?"

"I guess so."

"If a woman wanted to go to bed with you, what would be the best way for her to go about arranging it?"

Max felt a rush of blood to his face. He took a too-large gulp of the coffee, burning the roof of his mouth. Most of the women he'd been with in his life had been whores. And the few who hadn't been were never so direct about things. "I must be twice your age," he managed to say finally.

"Not quite. And what's that got to do with anything, anyway?"

Max didn't like conversations that got so personal. He made a point, had always made a point, of avoiding them. Part of the reason was survival, of course. In his line of work, the fewer people who knew about him and the less they knew, the better. But there was more to it than that, even. He was simply a private person, unused to expressing feelings or sharing much of himself with others. After so many years of being a solitary man Max wasn't sure that he would know how to get close to someone like Danni, even if he wanted to. Their worlds were too different.

How the hell had he allowed things to get to this point? Jesus, he was really slipping. He put the mug down carefully and reached for his wallet. "Better let me pay for that record and get out of here."

Danni bit her lower lip. After a moment she stood and went to the cash register. Neither spoke as they exchanged cash and album.

"See you next week," Max said as he headed for the door.

"Will you?" She sounded doubtful.

He managed a small smile. "Maybe you'll have the Powell by then."

"Maybe." She returned the smile, and Max left the store. He wasn't sure he'd really go back.

He lived in a loft that had once been part of a pillow factory. The first floor of the building was now an art gallery, operated by a guy named Paul Something, a Polish name that Max could never remember, even though he saw it every month on the rent checks the man gave him. The gallery itself specialized in Eastern European handicrafts. Max didn't mind the stuff; it surely beat some of the garbage that passed for art in many of the galleries in the area.

The loft was reached by a curved flight of heavy iron steps on the outside of the building. At the top of the stairs there was a small landing, and Max paused there to shift the packages he was holding and reach for the key.

Then he stopped, standing very still, not even breathing.

And wishing to hell that he had a gun.

Stupid, lazy old man.

The door wasn't closed all the way. After cursing himself roundly for perhaps thirty seconds Max considered just what to do next.

In that length of time he realized just how angry he was. No one had ever invaded his home before. No one had dared. Why did they now? Did they think that because Max Trueblood had quit working he would be an easy target? He got madder.

All that anger made him do the second stupid thing of the morning.

Max kicked the door open with one foot and charged inside. By all the rules of God and man he should have been dead almost immediately. But surprisingly, no one blasted him.

Two men were sitting on the large sofa that nearly filled one corner of the vast room. Max didn't know them. With his foot he pushed the door closed again. If they had been planning to kill him, they would have done it by now.

"What the hell are you doing in my place?" he asked quietly.

One of the men was black, wearing a gray suit that looked expensive and a narrow tie. His shoes gleamed. "Mr. Marberg sent us," he said in a voice that held a soft Jamaican accent.

"Is that supposed to mean something to me?" Max walked over to the counter that separated the living room from the kitchen and put his purchases down. As he moved, his gaze never left the two men.

The second intruder was a skinny redhead. "Mr. Marberg's name better mean something, old man," he said. His over-sized Adam's apple bobbed as he spoke.

A funny guy, Marberg. Only a man with a real sense of humor would team up the colored boy in the fancy clothes and this shit kicker who sounded about three hours out of Dixie. Max shook his head, smiling faintly. "Must be hard to get good help these days," he said. "Sam Marberg used to hire gorillas with manners." He took off his sunglasses, folded them, and put them down, safely out of the way. They were good glasses, expensive, and he didn't want them broken if anything happened. And maybe something was going to happen.

Red wanted very much to say something, but he was stopped by a warning look from the other man. The lump in his throat bobbed again as he swallowed the comment.

"Mr. Marberg wants to see you," the Jamaican said. "He sent us to get you."

"To get me?" Max thought about that for a moment, then decided that he didn't like the implication much. Instead of telling them that, however, he just started unpacking the produce. "Nice tomatoes today," he commented. "That Viet guy gets good stuff." He walked over to the fridge and put the fruit and vegetables away in the crisper. Before closing the door, he took out a beer. He didn't offer his visitors anything. "Uh, listen, uh—"

"Donald," the Islander said.

"Donald. Good. I like to know who it is I'm inviting to get the hell out of my place."

"That might not be the wise thing for you to do."

Max murmured an Italian obscenity, which, since this was New York, both the Jamaican and the hillbilly seemed to understand.

Donald only smiled a little, but his partner turned a mottled pink color that clashed with his hair. "We don't have to take this shit from a prick like you."

"You don't have to do a damned thing except leave."

"The boss ain't gonna like this."

"I don't really care one way or the other what he does or doesn't like. He's your boss, boys, not mine."

Donald listened to the exchange, then shook his head in apparent dismay. "We're only doing a job, man." Except that when he said it, the word came out *mon*.

Max opened a cupboard to take out a heavy glass mug, then he walked over to the dining table and sat down. "See, that's the difference between you and me. One of them, anyway. I don't work for Marberg now. I don't work for anybody, because I'm retired. Which means that I don't have to put up with aggravation like this anymore."

Red sneered. "I don't know why the boss wants to see you, anyway. Old man."

Max smiled. "Probably he wants me because I'm very good. And there isn't anybody around as good today." He let his gaze move over them slowly, at the same time dropping one hand and slipping it under the long, fringed serape that served as a tablecloth. "At least, he doesn't seem to have anybody that good on his payroll."

Once again Donald stopped the other man with a glance. "You should come talk to him. You owe him that much, at least."

"I don't owe Sam Marberg or anybody else a goddamned thing. I always gave full measure to the people I worked for. Now I'm retired. He should know that already, but maybe you boys better remind him." Max poured the beer. "Ever have a Taddy Porter? Looks like Coke, doesn't it? A good

brew. But sort of costly. Maybe after you fellows work for
Marberg or somebody just like Marberg for forty years, you'll
be able to afford it. If you live that long."

As Max spoke the final words he brought his hand out from
under the serape. In it he held a .357 Combat revolver. He
pointed it at Red. "That's a handy little shelf I built under this
table. Guess you didn't notice it because of the fancy Mexican
cloth. Nice gun, too, right? Just in case your vocational
training classes didn't mention it, this particular weapon holds
six bullets. And the last time I tried, I could still get them off
pretty fast. Fast enough, anyway."

"You are being very foolish," Donald said.

"Well, when a man gets to be my age, he's entitled. Now
get the hell out of here. Tell Marberg that the next time he
sends a couple of half-assed punks around here to bother me,
he just might get them back in a slightly damaged condition.
If at all. Got that?"

Donald tipped his head in a slight nod. "We will deliver the
message." He stood slowly, careful not to make any sudden
moves that a man with a gun might misinterpret, and after a
moment Red followed suit.

"This ain't nowhere's near finished, old man."

Max smiled again but didn't say anything. The barrel of the
revolver followed them across the room and out the door. He
got up quickly and threw all three locks into place. After a few
seconds he could hear the pounding of their feet going down
the stairs.

Only then did he replace the gun on the shelf.

He put the Charlie Parker on the stereo, turning the
volume up high. Paul Whatever downstairs never complained
about the noise. When all the fancy dials on the machine were
set to their best advantage, Max sat down with the Taddy
Porter again.

It was enough to make a man thoughtful.

two:

success story

1

Kasdan didn't believe him at first.

The attorney just looked at him from the other side of the big glass-topped desk and smiled. The smile wore a nasty edge. "Mr. Tadzio doesn't meet with the hired help," he said.

"Is that why he has you?" Jeremiah responded.

Then he bit his tongue. Damn, don't alienate him. Jeremiah didn't like lawyers, or guys who talked like they'd been to Yale, especially when he knew damned well that Erik Kasdan had grown up in Brooklyn and graduated from NYU. But right now he needed the bastard. Idiot that he was, the lawyer was his only direct pipeline to Tadzio.

So he smiled to cover the crack and didn't complain about the label of "hired help." Which, strictly speaking, he supposed was true. For the time being, at least. "Couldn't you just pass along the message that I'd like to meet with him? He's missing out on a good bet if he won't at least do that much."

Kasdan took a cigarette from a slender silver case, not offering him one. "A good bet? By which, I suppose, you mean yourself?"

11

"Damned right. Look, Kasdan, I'm wasted where I am now." Which was mostly nowhere, they both knew, but nobody said so.

"A small-time crook with ambition. That could be dangerous."

Jeremiah shook his head. "I'm not dangerous, for chrissake. All I am is a man who wants a chance. Just a try for my cut of the good life, like they talk about in the beer commercials. I've been out in the trenches for a fucking long time, Kasdan."

It seemed like forever, in fact, and he was tired of it. Tired of being paid out of petty cash. Of living like a loser. Jeremiah leaned forward a little in the chair. "Didn't I come through when Mr. Tadzio needed me? Twice?" There was no need for him to cite specifics; Kasdan knew damned well what he was talking about.

Kasdan was quiet as he smoked the cigarette and leaned back to stare at the ceiling. Finally he came forward and looked at Jeremiah. "Okay, Donahue. It's just barely possible that you might have a valid point."

Barely fucking possible. The bastard. He could remember when Erik Kasdan, Esq., was running all over the city carrying numbers slips in a brown paper sack.

But Jeremiah kept a smile on his face.

"Flash and ambition," Kasdan said. "It might work out to everybody's advantage. Let me see what I can do. No promises, you understand, but I'll talk to Mr. Tadzio and find out what he thinks. We all remember the good work you did on those two occasions."

Jeremiah let his stomach muscles relax for the first time since he'd come into Kasdan's office. He was over the first hurdle.

He was on his way.

The meeting with Kasdan had been two days ago, and tonight it was about to pay off. His big chance had arrived.

And it was better than he'd ever dared to hope for. Instead

of only having a chance to talk to the top man, he was actually having dinner with Raphael Tadzio. Jeremiah still couldn't quite believe it. All he knew for sure was that this dinner was his best chance ever to grab at the gold ring, and that he'd better not screw it up. Opportunity had been a helluva long time knocking.

It was for that reason he'd gone out and spent almost his last red cent on new clothes. Appearance was important when you were dealing with somebody like Tadzio. Like what it said in that book about dressing right to be a success. Maybe clothes didn't exactly make the man, but they sure as hell helped.

After considerable thought he'd decided to go with the classic look. Nothing flashy; the man should make the real impact, not his clothes. Blue blazer with gold buttons. The buttons had little ships on them. Gray slacks. Pale blue Oxford shirt. And, for the first time in his life, a real silk tie. Now he was practically broke, with not even enough money to pay the rent, but if this dinner panned out the way he hoped, that wouldn't matter. Pretty soon the big money would be his.

As he dressed, he listened to his favorite Beach Boys album.

Listening to the music made him realize that the old surfing poster on the wall was starting to look a little faded to him. Like everything else around here lately, including his dreams. So maybe it was time to get a new poster and some new dreams.

The broad next door started in on practicing her damned opera right on time. Jesus, he hadda get out of this crummy room, out of the whole crummy neighborhood. Maybe he was too old for the beaches of Malibu—okay, no maybe about it, he was too old for that kind of escape—but there were other places, other dreams.

He hit the wall with the heel of one hand. "Shut the hell up," he yelled at the woman.

"Go fuck yourself," she replied, not missing a beat.

They went through this same routine almost every day.

Jeremiah stood in front of the mirror to finish knotting the tie. It took two tries to get the Windsor right, but finally it was perfect. He admired himself in the cracked glass. All in all, not bad, even if he was the only one around to say so. Except that maybe the hair was a little long. He ran a hand through the tangled curls. Too late to worry about that now.

Next door the broad hit her high note. Jeremiah walked over to his stereo and jacked up the volume on "Good Vibrations." Then he sat on the edge of the sofa bed to slip on and tie the new black shoes. The glossy leather was so bright that he could see his face.

As far as he could see, there was nothing here that Tadzio wouldn't approve of for one of his top soldiers.

It was almost time to leave; he didn't want to risk getting caught in traffic and being late. Punctuality was important. He opened the top drawer of the dresser and stared down at the holster there. The gun was new, too, just like the blazer. He'd never owned one before, but it had seemed like the right thing to buy the weapon now. Still, he was nervous about actually putting it on and going out onto the street. Jeremiah was aware that there was a certain bizarre humor in the way he felt. He was a man who could deal easily with dynamite or plastic explosives, but guns were different. He didn't know why, but they were.

The bitch let out a screech that sounded like somebody was raping her. Fat chance of that ever happening, of course. A man would have to be pretty desperate before he'd want to dip his rod into that ugly blimp.

Jeremiah slid the small blue steel pistol out of its holster and hefted it thoughtfully. Then he aimed it at the wall. "Die, you bitch," he said tightly, pretending to pull the trigger. "Bang, bang, bang." He grinned.

Yeah, so maybe he wasn't too thrilled about walking around the city with a guaranteed trip inside strapped under his arm, but what if Tadzio asked him if he was carrying? It wouldn't look good to say no. Be prepared.

So he slipped the gun back into the black leather holster, put it on, then donned the blazer and examined himself critically in the mirror again. Nothing showed. Nobody could tell he was carrying. Except him.

He took one more look into the mirror, smiled, and stood where he was long enough for Brian and Dennis and the boys to finish one last song.

Then he left the room.

He ended up getting to the restaurant too early. Nerves had made him hurry. But since he was there, he went on in. The tuxedo-clad stiff at the front desk eyed him with suspicion, not seeming to be very impressed by the new clothes. Jeremiah didn't give a damn; he hadn't dressed to impress this foreign fag, anyway.

He was willing to bet that if the fairy saw the gun under his blazer, he'd be impressed okay. Probably piss his fancy pants.

Since Mr. Tadzio hadn't arrived yet, Jeremiah was directed into the bar to wait.

One thing he couldn't afford to do was get drunk; he knew that, but at the same time he decided that a little alcoholic courage couldn't hurt. When a man was waiting for the most important meeting of his life, he wanted all systems on go. It would really be a bitch to look back years later and realize that his entire life had been fucked up because he'd worn the wrong tie or downed one too many beers or anything else that dumb.

He ordered a shot and a beer, then fingered the tie thoughtfully. No fear about this. It was great, a sort of regimental stripe in blue and red. He swiveled to catch sight of himself in the glass partition and practiced looking confident.

When the drinks were set in front of him, he downed the shot in one gulp, grimacing a little at the taste, then took a soothing sip of the Heineken. The conversation around him was muted, suiting the dignity of the red velvet and gold room. Fancy stuff. So this was where the rich folks drank. He thought that he could get used to it with very little effort.

Not much like the old Spotted Dog Bar and Grill in Hoboken.

But he put that thought behind him quickly. This was no time to let the past come creeping up and surprise him. Jeremiah Donahue had been on the hustle forever, since those long-ago days when he and his mother lived above the Spotted Dog, and now was the time for all his work and waiting to pay off.

The soft tap on his shoulder startled him. He jerked around and saw the penguin from the front standing there. "Mr. Tadzio has arrived, sir. He asked that I show you to his table." The creep didn't sound like he thought that was a very good idea.

Jeremiah nodded. He gulped down the rest of the beer, then carefully wiped his mouth on the little paper napkin. "Ready," he said.

The man led him out of the bar, through a large dining room crowded with people, without stopping. They went up a wide, carpeted staircase and into a much smaller room. There were only four tables here, two of which were empty. The third was occupied by a pair of guys he didn't know but who looked like out-of-shape wrestlers crammed into cheap suits. Definitely not dressed for success, those two. They were drinking beer from bottles.

Tadzio and Kasdan were at the other table. Jeremiah crossed the room and, at Tadzio's nod, sat down. The boss didn't say anything, because he was involved in tasting some wine. Everybody else stayed quiet, too, as if they were in some kind of Twilight Zone of suspended animation. The old man made a show of it. When he finally nodded in satisfaction, the waiter filled three glasses.

Jeremiah still waited, not sure what was the right thing to

do now. Was he supposed to speak, or wait until he was spoken to? He glanced at Kasdan, but the bastard only looked right back at him, his eyes hard to read behind the glasses. The lawyer seemed to be enjoying Jeremiah's discomfort.

Tadzio drank some of the wine. "Glad you could make it tonight," he said at last.

"Thank you," Jeremiah said. His voice sounded a little shaky, so he lubricated his throat with a swallow of the wine. It was too sweet.

"I like to get business out of the way first," Tadzio said. "Makes the food go down better."

"Fine."

"So tell me, Donahue, how long have you been with the organization?"

"Since I was fifteen." Said out loud like that, it sounded like an eternity, and he felt old all of a sudden.

"That's a long time. You started out in Jersey, am I right?"

Jeremiah had the feeling that Tadzio knew all of this very well, and probably a lot more besides, but if this was the way the game was played, he would go along. "I was a runner in Hoboken."

"So many years. That's good. I like a loyal man. Loyal people make for a strong company." Tadzio smiled broadly as the waiter delivered a massive antipasto platter and set it in the center of the table. "Nice, huh? They do this up special for me when I come in." He switched gears abruptly, turning to Kasdan. "Tell me, Erik, what kind of reports do we get on Donahue?"

Kasdan had just picked up a piece of cheese. He didn't eat it immediately, opting instead to answer Tadzio. "Fine reports, sir. Always fine." He sounded sincere, and he probably was, because he had suggested this meet, maybe even pressed for it a little, and if it worked out well, he could take the credit. "You remember, sir, how well he performed on the Alphonse matter. And Willy Ngo—that was Jerry too."

Jeremiah was interested to see that Kasdan lost a little of his arrogant edge in Tadzio's company. Maybe he was a big-shot lawyer, but he was also one of the boss's flunkies. That thought took a few of the butterflies out of Jeremiah's gut.

"Good work on those things," Tadzio said. "They say you're one of the best we have for that kind of job."

"Probably that's true," Jeremiah said. "But I'm tired of just blowing up cars."

Tadzio seemed amused. "You are?"

"A man likes to try new things," Jeremiah responded. He shrugged. "Maybe get where the big money is, the steady money, you know?"

"Ever been arrested?" Tadzio asked. "And I got friends on the department, so don't try to bullshit me."

Jeremiah set the wineglass down and rested his palms on the tablecloth. "Couple times when I was a kid," he said, managing to sound offhanded about it. "Small stuff. Curfew. Joyriding. Once, DWI. One shoplifting rap that was dismissed. Nothing else."

"That's good. Maybe you're smart or maybe you're just lucky."

Jeremiah was starting to feel good. He smiled. "Maybe I'm both," he said.

"Maybe." Tadzio took a moment to devote his attention to the antipasto.

Jeremiah looked at the greasy platter, but he didn't take anything. His stomach was still so knotted up that just the smell of olive oil was threatening. It would be ultra-uncool to puke all over the godfather.

Kasdan finally finished the damned cheese; he cleared his throat. "I think that Donahue might be ready to move up within the company. We could use him to advantage, in my opinion."

Tadzio wiped at the dribble of oil coursing down his chin. "Yeah? You think? Well, lemme tell you something, Jerry. There's a lot going on in the business at this particular time."

"I heard that."

"You heard that, didja?" Tadzio eyed him for a moment. "What do we got here? Something more than just a good explosives man? You really are a smart boy, huh, Donahue?"

"And lucky," he said.

There was another pause before Tadzio smiled faintly. "Maybe I like you, Jerry. Yeah, just maybe I do. You got hustle and you got brains. And most important, you got what they call initiative. Initiative is what made this country great. You know what that means?"

Jeremiah nodded.

"Initiative," Tadzio went on, anyway, "means that you had the moxie to ask for this meet. Not many guys do that. Plus, you got some style." He glanced across the room to where the two losers were sitting. "Style, that's good these days. So I think we can say there's a place for you. In fact, I got a special project coming up immediately that I think you might be just the boy for. What do you think, Erik? Jerry, here, right for that job we were talking about before?"

"Yes, sir, I think so. He's proved himself."

"Yeah, I know. Alphonse and the chink." Tadzio studied him. "It's not gonna be easy, this new job, Jerry. But are you interested?"

Jeremiah bit back a triumphant shout. "Sure," he said coolly. "I'm very interested. Whatever you want, Mr. Tadzio, I'm the one for the job."

Tadzio peered at him another moment, then nodded. "No more business now. Now we eat."

Jeremiah reached for his wineglass.

2

He jumped from the bus for the three-block walk back to his apartment, feeling like a man who had finally figured out the secret of the good life. No more crap for him.

The residents of the neighborhood all seemed to be hanging out on the stoops and sidewalks; it was too hot to stay inside the cramped apartments. Six or seven boys showing gang colors huddled on the corner, passing around a joint and a bottle of Ripple. Jeremiah crossed Tenth Street to avoid them.

The super, a big Cuban who claimed to have been a secret policeman for Batista, was in the lobby. He glanced up from the racing form as Jeremiah passed, but didn't say anything.

Friendly place.

The first thing he did when he got upstairs was to take off his new clothes and hang them carefully back in the closet. There was no sense in getting them all wrinkled and sweaty. He might need them for the job Tadzio had promised him.

He pulled on a pair of jeans that had been hacked off above the knees, grabbed a beer, and crawled out onto the fire escape.

"There you are," said a voice from above.

He craned his neck and looked upward. "Hi, Sandy."

She climbed down the ladder and landed next to him. "What'd you have, a big night or something?"

"Why?"

"I saw you come in all prettied up. You looked like one of those newsmen on the television."

"Yeah, well, I guess you could say I had a big night."

"Why?"

"I had a business dinner with one of the most important men in the city. Maybe even in the whole country."

She looked properly impressed with that. "Why was somebody like that having dinner with you?"

He swallowed some beer and shrugged. "The man wanted to offer me a job. A real great opportunity."

Her expression turned a little skeptical. "Uh-huh."

He frowned a little. Nobody was going to take the glow off this evening, not even Sandy. "So how come you're home so early? The streets didn't run out of tricks, did they?"

She didn't take offense but only waved a hand in front of her face. "Too hot for screwing."

Sandy, which probably wasn't her real name, was pretty in a ruined sort of way. Short red hair, vague green eyes, and a body that was nice enough to almost make up for the shortage of brainpower. She hooked, of course, but since they were friends, after a fashion, Jeremiah scored an occasional freebie.

He didn't like the fact that she did drugs, but then that wasn't really any of his business. Once, under her persuasion, he'd tried some coke, but only once. Drugs scared him. Losers were the only ones who swallowed, smoked, or needled crap into themselves. Dumb shits who weren't going anywhere except to the grave.

Not Jeremiah Padraic Donahue. He was a winner.

He handed her the rest of the beer. "Finish this." When he returned with a new can for himself, she was leaning over the railing, idly watching a fight in the street below. "What's this new job, Jerry?"

He hated the nickname, but people always seemed determined to use it. Easier to accept it than to fight the same battle a dozen times a week. "Well, I won't know the details until tomorrow." He drank. "Some special project was all he said."

"Well, you got the brains for it. Didn't I always say that?"

He smiled.

There was something very sad about Sandy. She was one of those losers going no place. If the drugs didn't kill her soon, some crazy trick probably would. Once, deep into a bottle of cheap red wine, it had occurred to him that maybe Sandy got to him because something in the wounded eyes reminded him of his mother. But that thought was troubling for reasons he didn't understand, so he pushed it aside.

He leaned in through the window and punched the stereo on. The Mamas and Papas blasted out, sounding sweet and drowning out the noisy Latin beat coming from someplace else in the building.

They sat quietly for a time, just drinking beer and listening. Sandy asked him for maybe the hundredth time or so why he didn't ever play any Prince stuff. He just sneered. Although he kept trying to explain good music to her, the broad was just too stupid to learn.

Finally they moved inside to the bed.

It really was, as she had said, too hot for any heavy action, but they fooled around a little, anyway, just because he felt like celebrating and she was always willing. She gave him one of her standard twenty-dollar blow jobs.

Jeremiah wasn't really thinking about it. After all, he had important things on his mind. Like what Tadzio would say to him in the morning. And what the job would turn out to be.

The record clicked off, and a few minutes later Sandy got up from the bed and left, using the door this time. Jeremiah got up only long enough to put a Gene Pitney album on the stereo and to splash cold water over himself. Then he adjusted the flow of the cheap fan so that it would blow directly on him, and stretched out on the bed again.

After a lifetime of going second-class, of getting close but never quite making it to the big one, he could sense that everything was about to change. It was a little scary, he had to admit, but it was also pretty damned exciting.

Thinking about it kept him awake most of the night.

three:

film at eleven

1

Aaron Temple was getting tired of death. He was just fed up with being forced, day in and day out, to look at, ponder upon, and investigate the recently deceased. It didn't make him feel any better to remember—was it from Hemingway?—that the dead were tired too.

How many bodies had he seen over the last four decades? There was no way of figuring the exact count, even if he really wanted to, but whatever the tally, this morning it was definitely too many by at least one. Absently, he shifted the unlit cigar to the other side of his mouth. Since the damned doctor had cut him down to two a day, he tried not to light the first one until after lunch. On days like this, though, such restraint was a struggle.

After another quick glance at the body propped against the rear of the bodega, Aaron looked around for his partner. A small crowd had gathered on Ninety-sixth Street, just a couple of bored beat cops mingling with a few abnormally curious locals. For most of the citizens of this neighborhood the discovery of one more body was only a ripple in the day.

Just a moment before Aaron would have felt justified in

23

letting his impatience show, Cody Blaine appeared from wherever he'd been skulking. He was drinking a can of Coke Classic, probably charmed for nothing out of the bodega owner, a small but very fat woman who was loudly expressing her anger at this disruption in her business. The body was an annoyance, and the nosy cops pests. It didn't surprise Aaron that despite her surly mood, Blaine could still sweet-talk her out of a soda. He was wasted on the police payroll. A man like that could go far in politics.

As usual Blaine looked more like a down-at-the-heels actor than a homicide dick. Aaron could remember when being a detective meant wearing a suit and tie every day, and to him it still did. Cody, however, must have missed that class at the academy. Today he had turned up in a bright yellow T-shirt and faded jeans. A holster hung under one arm, the huge gun it held naked for all the world to see. It didn't look like he'd taken time to shave.

The funny thing was, Aaron liked the younger man, anyway. They'd been partnered for about a year now, ever since Blaine came onto the squad, a hotshot out of Vice with a record-setting arrest and conviction rate. As well as a rep as a hotdogger in some quarters. Aaron, at first nonplussed by being teamed with Blaine, now figured that he couldn't find anybody better with whom to spend his last days as a cop. Once you got past the clothes and the admittedly irreverent attitude, what you had was a damned good cop. Aaron didn't think that anything else mattered much.

It was simple: Even in this age of dirty cops and dirtier crime, Cody Blaine just plain loved the job as much as Aaron always had.

Blaine finally strolled over to grace the scene with his presence. He took a gulp of the Coke and stared glumly at the body. "Whaddaya think, Aaron?" His partner, thank God, wasn't one of those new-breed know-it-alls who thought that there was nothing at all to be learned by listening to a fossil.

Aaron moved his gaze back to the figure on the ground. The

man's hands were tied behind his back, and there was a silver-dollar-sized hole through the middle of his head. It was too hot for September, which meant that a body didn't have to sit around too long before it started to offend. "Well," Aaron said slowly, "I think the son of a bitch is probably dead."

Blaine choked briefly on the Coke, then aimed his Pepsodent bright molars at him. "You're probably right about that. You oughtta be a fucking detective."

"I also think that this is the third in a series," Aaron continued more soberly. "And three of a kind in less than two weeks begins to look significant. This is starting to feel like an all-out family war."

The prospect seemed to delight Blaine. He crushed the flimsy soda pop can with one hand and absently tossed it toward the already overflowing trash bin. "War," he said softly, sounding strangely reverent.

Aaron, however, had been around the mob and their battles for a very long time. He wasn't entirely thrilled by the prospect of closing out his career by tangling with the same old bunch he'd been dealing with since the forties.

Still and all, it might beat the crowd they had to cope with these days. The druggies. The Colombian dealers who would wipe out a whole family if one member dared to cross them. The psychos who seemed to crawl out of the woodwork of the city with increasing and depressing regularity. At least a man knew where he stood with the pros.

"This should be right up your alley, Aaron," Cody said, nudging him in the ribs.

That was true. Aaron Temple knew all the ins and outs of organized crime in the city better than anybody else still with the department, even those big-deal college boys that were popping up everywhere these days. He'd been studying the bastards for years, after all. Too many years, according to the assholes in charge. He was almost sixty-five now, within months of a retirement that he didn't want but that he would take before being forced into some damned desk job. It wasn't fair. Okay, he had a bum leg, but beyond that he was doing good. And the mind—the mind was as sharp as ever.

But did the damned bureaucrats care about that? And why should they, when half of them were probably on the payroll of the bosses? No wonder the move was on to get rid of Aaron Temple.

So to hell with them. He wasn't retired yet, and until he was, he'd keep right on doing what he'd been doing since what felt like back around the Stone Age: working to clear the scum off the streets of his city. That was what he knew how to do best, all he knew how to do, actually. And it didn't matter to him whether the scumbags he busted wore jeans and carried Saturday night specials or dressed in three-piece suits and defended themselves with a battery of Harvard lawyers. Garbage was garbage.

He sighed and started back toward the car, ignoring the catcalls and smartass remarks of the leftover whores and hopheads. Time to let the scientific boys do their shtick. He could wait to read all the pretty little details in their neatly typed report. He knew everything it would say, anyway.

Blaine followed him, then slid behind the wheel of their battered Ford. "So this guy was connected?" he said, lighting a cigarette. He finished off at least three packs a day, blithely ignoring both the best advice of the medical community and the increasing hostility of the general populace.

Aaron nodded. "His name was Paco Smith. He was a minor cog in the wheel as cogs go, but he was definitely connected. Last I heard, he was running a string of broads and dealing a little."

Cody started the car, then glanced over at him through a cloud of gray smoke. "What the hell do you think is going on here? Why so much action all of a sudden?"

"Damned if I know. Maybe all the indictments the feds have been handing down are shaking the power structure. Wish I did know, because running two steps behind these creeps makes me nervous." Aaron decided to light the damned stogie and be done with it. It was almost noon, anyway.

"Well, whatever it is, we'll track it down," Cody said confidently.

Youth was a wonderful thing, even if it did get a little irritating sometimes. Aaron shrugged, fumbling for a match. "Let's take an early lunch," he said, mostly to salve his conscience over lighting up so early. "I got a taste for pastrami."

Aaron still lived in the same small house in Brooklyn that he'd bought right after his marriage in 1948. He lived there alone, as he had since 1955 and his divorce. He liked the house, and after a few years he'd started to like living alone. It was easier.

Tonight, however, nothing seemed easy.

The rotten morning had evolved into a very long and mostly worthless afternoon, and he was tired, so when he turned the corner and saw the dark blue Saab parked in his driveway, he sighed. Company was something he definitely didn't need tonight, especially not this particular company. He fleetingly considered just driving on by, going someplace for a drink or two, hoping that the unwelcome visitor would get tired of waiting and leave.

But he knew that she wouldn't.

So he bowed to the inevitable, parked on the street, and went inside to get it over with.

She was polishing the furniture in the small, square living room, using that stuff that left the place smelling like sticky lemonade. Aaron took off his jacket and hung it on the doorknob.

"Actually," he said, "I like a little dust. Makes a room feel lived in."

Susan jumped at the sound of his voice, then turned. She had obviously come directly from work, because she was still wearing the neat gray suit and white blouse. Susan was what the *Times* kept calling a yuppie. At thirty-five she was already a partner in a successful young advertising firm, not to mention that she was married to an up-and-coming corporate attorney. Together they had produced a child, now three, a girl, who was at the top of her nursery school class.

Susan was Aaron's daughter.

Because of the bitter divorce he had not seen her at all from the age of five until she was twenty years older. Maybe he had missed her early on, although the job had kept him so busy that he didn't really know her—and how well could one know a five-year-old, anyway? But by the time she reappeared in his life, he didn't need to have his landscape cluttered up by family. Susan felt differently about it, however. She was determined that they were going to be the perfect father and daughter. Aaron had the feeling that she cared less about him as a person than about the notion of an ideal family. She could not bear to fail in any aspect of her life. He was part of the image.

She annoyed the hell out of him.

Not to mention that her husband was a pompous ass and the kid a spoiled brat.

Susan gave the coffee table another rub. "You really need to keep things up, Dad, so when you sell, you'll get as good a price as possible."

He wasn't up to debating the sale of his house with her, not after the day he'd had, so he just went into the kitchen for a beer. She had already been in that room. The dirty dishes were gone, and a pot of something was bubbling on the stove. He sniffed suspiciously. "What's that?"

"Lamb stew."

He hated lamb in any form, and he wasn't crazy about stew, either. "I was planning on having franks 'n' beans for supper."

"This is better for you."

He sat at the table, putting the beer can down on the oilcloth and wishing that he had taken Cody up on his suggestion that they grab a steak downtown. He had refused because he knew that the younger cop just wanted to talk about the killings, and he was too whacked out. But now, rehashing a couple of murders with Cody seemed highly preferable to this.

Susan joined him at the table. She was drinking a glass of white wine. "Dad, have you started the retirement papers yet?"

"Soon. What are you rushing me for?"

Her tone was sweet reason. "I'm not rushing you. It's just that we need to make plans."

"We? I thought that you were making all the plans around here."

She put on what he thought of as her let's-humor-poor-old-Dad face. "Well, I can see that you're in a rotten mood tonight."

He shrugged. "I'm tired. We got a stiff today that looks like three of a kind. I think that all hell is about to break loose among the crime families."

"That shouldn't concern you now."

"It shouldn't?" He looked at her for a moment, then shook his head. "Cody, my partner, he's all excited. I think he must've watched *The Untouchables* too much when he was a boy."

"If he's so excited, let him face the criminals for a change. You're done with that."

"Not yet, I'm not, missy," he said sharply. "I'll be the one to say when I'm done. Cody's good, but he's not ready for this yet. He needs my help."

"You're stalling, Dad."

"Stalling? That's your word for it. Maybe I'm just not done living my life yet."

She set the wine down. "You're too old for this kind of thing. You could get killed."

Aaron took a long sip of beer, then lowered the can and stared at her. "Maybe. But also maybe that wouldn't be the worst way to go."

"That's a terrible thing to say."

Aaron couldn't remember anymore what her mother had looked like or if he'd loved her. He thought back, trying to recall committing the act that led to this woman being made, and that, too, was lost in the past. Maybe he had loved his wife, certainly he had impregnated her; but did that mean that now this stranger had the right to come in here and start running his life? He had to fight back, but dammit, he was tired. "Why is that so terrible? Dying in the line of duty sure beats vegetating to death out in Westchester." He smiled. "Besides, like I said, my partner is good. He'll back me up."

Susan stood. "We'll talk another day. You're in a real mood."

When she was gone, Aaron turned off the gas flame under the lamb stew. He opened the fridge and took out a pan of leftover franks and beans.

While they heated, he opened another beer and read the *News.*

2

Even though Aaron had turned him down on dinner, Cody didn't go straight home. In fact, he found himself doing that less and less lately. It just seemed as if there were always something better to do. Something more interesting. Even if it was only having dinner with Aaron and talking about work. Or on nights like this one, when he was left on his own, he could run down a snitch from his days on Vice and see what the grapevine was whispering about.

Sometimes he would reinterview a witness or two.

But neither of those options appealed to him tonight.

He knew that going home was the smart thing to do. So many late nights was earning him a lot of flak, but there were things a cop had to do if he wanted to be good.

And Cody Blaine wanted to be the best. He wanted to rise

way above the pack of ordinary cops. The path to glory was a tricky one, he knew, full of chuckholes and traps, but he had it figured out. What he had to do was be as good a cop as Aaron Temple and a helluva lot better politician. That was where old Aaron had blown it over the years. He never knew how to play the political games in the department.

Or, if he knew how, chose not to play.

Whatever.

But Cody knew that he was smarter than that. And more ambitious. Ambition meant hard work and long hours, and if other people, namely Amanda, couldn't understand that, it was just tough.

So tonight, instead of going home after they signed out, he headed for a place called Jo-Jo's. Somebody, one of his junkie snitches, he thought, had once told him that a lot of mob guys hung out there. Wouldn't he just love to uncover some lead that he could hand to Aaron? He knew that his partner would put the credit where it was due, and that could only help his rep within the department.

He donned the wrinkled blue sportcoat retrieved from the back of the VW and lit a cigarette before going into the bar. Tried not to look like a cop.

His first thought was that if this joint was a Mafia hangout, it was something of a disappointment. There were seven or eight men sitting around the circular bar, and if they were an example of hotshot crime figures, things were rough for the bad guys. These turkeys looked like rejects from something.

Still, you never knew.

Cody took a place at the bar. "Soda," he said. "With a twist."

The bartender made another swipe at the counter with a dirty rag. "Big drinker," he said. "Big spender."

Cody just smiled.

When the glass was in front of him, he took a careful sip. "Terrific," he said. "You make a good drink, Ernie." The name was stitched on the front of his puce bowling shirt.

"Yeah, well, water with lemon skin floating in it is one of my specialties."

"Lucky that's what I wanted, then, isn't it?"

Ernie snorted and moved away.

Cody didn't drink liquor. Couldn't drink it. What he had was some kind of weird allergy to alcohol in any form. He didn't really mind not being able to booze it up, but he did think that it sometimes put a crimp in his style. It had been worse when he worked Vice.

He swiveled slowly on the bar stool, his gaze running the length of the room. There was nobody in here who looked even vaguely interesting. They were all talking sports or broads, but nobody was saying anything about dead gangsters.

So much for his one-man crusade against crime. Oh, well, at least he hadn't told Aaron what he planned to do. The old bastard would have gotten a real chuckle out of it, probably.

Cody finished his drink and decided that he might as well go home. He'd only be an hour or so late, which in the greater scheme of things was hardly worth arguing about. And maybe he'd be really lucky and Mandy would have worked late.

Disgusted with both the bar and himself, he tossed Ernie a quarter tip and left.

four:

rock 'n' roll will
never die

1

Max ordered another beer from Madge, the overweight barmaid. He didn't actually say anything to her; all he had to do was catch her eye and nod. That was a benefit of being a regular in the Dying Swan.

The bar was something of an anachronism in the area. There was nothing even slightly trendy about either the Swan itself or its clientele, which consisted mostly of the old-time, stubborn hangers-on of the neighborhood. The Swan was their place, and they gathered there nightly, much as the English do in their local pubs, which is actually what the Dying Swan resembled. Max liked it much more than any of the fern and wine places springing up all around. He used the bar as a sort of refuge whenever the solitude of his loft became oppressive rather than comforting. There was a large television, used for sporting events of all kinds, *Wheel of Fortune*, and sometimes *M*A*S*H* reruns. There was also a traditional dartboard.

Max didn't play darts, and he rarely looked at the television unless Lasorda's Bums were playing. And, unlike many of the bar's patrons, he didn't come in every night. Usually he limited himself to two nights a week, but he enjoyed it, appreciating the fact that a man could have a couple of drinks, read, relax as he wanted, and not be bothered by anyone.

Usually.

He turned another page in the paperback novel, frowning a little. There was a new face in the Swan tonight, which was unusual enough in itself. Even stranger was the fact that the newcomer didn't fit the profile of the basic Swan customer. He was too young, for one thing, and he was wearing a pink knit shirt, something which had probably never been seen before inside the walls of this place.

But beyond all that, Max had the distinct feeling that whoever the unknown face belonged to was watching him with unseemly curiosity. After several minutes of this, Max struck back. Without tipping his hand he made use of the mirror behind the bar to study the stranger.

A kid, somewhere in his twenties if appearance could be trusted, with curly brown hair and the slick manner of a con man. And without a doubt a pretty damned good con man, because who could resist the dimple, visible even at this distance, whenever he smiled? Which he did with annoying frequency it seemed to Max, but whether it was at Madge as she flirted or at the television or maybe just at some private joke wasn't clear.

What was clear was that Max had been right: Although he was trying to be very subtle about it, the kid was definitely watching him. Fleetingly, Max thought about just leaving, going home, but then he decided that it would be smarter to hang around and see just what the hell was going on. Closing the book, he wrapped both hands around the beer mug and waited.

It didn't take long.

The smiler slid from the bar stool. He tugged at the edge of the damned alligator shirt, ran a hand through the curls, and strolled with almost painful casualness back to Max's booth.

"Excuse me, sir," he said in a quiet, polite voice.

Max looked directly at him for the first time. "What?"

"You're Max Trueblood, right?"

Since the visit by the two goons the day before, Max had worn a small ankle gun. Under the table he crossed one leg over the other, putting a hand on his calf. "I might be. If it's any of your business. Is it any of your business who I am?"

The dimple appeared. "Well, maybe not. But I just wanted to meet you."

"Why?"

"Because . . . I've heard of you is all."

Whether the obvious embarrassment was real or part of the act would have been hard to say. If it was phony, it was well done, but then it would have been from this one. Max studied him for a moment. "Sit down," he said finally, leaving his hand where it was near the gun.

"Lemme get my beer," the other man said. He hurried back to the bar, picked up the mug, then returned to the booth.

"Sit right there," Max ordered, pointing at exactly the correct spot. From here he could put a shot right between the friendly blue eyes if it became necessary. "You have a name?"

"Donahue. Jeremiah Donahue."

It meant nothing to him. Max used his free hand to lift the beer and take a sip, his eyes on Donahue's face. "You say you've heard of me. Where?"

"Oh, around."

"Wrong answer, Jeremiah." Max smiled.

Red crept up Donahue's cheeks. He wet his mouth with some beer. Nerves? "Well, a guy gets around," he said, sounding defensive. "I know some people. Maybe I've done a few things. You know how it goes."

"Do I?"

"Your name has come up over the years. People speak highly of you." Donahue seemed to get impatient or maybe angry all of a sudden. He set the mug down with a crash. "Hey, man, let's forget it, huh?" He stood. "I just saw you sitting here. Somebody pointed you out to me once a long time ago. I thought maybe we could talk. Sorry as all hell for bothering you."

He stalked back to his bar stool and hunched there, staring at the television screen as he viciously crushed peanuts.

Max sat still, patting his leg thoughtfully. Finally he raised a hand to summon Madge.

She came right over; he always tipped well. "What can I do for you, Max?"

"You want to tell Mr. Coverboy over there that he forgot his beer?"

Donahue listened, expressionless, as Madge delivered the message. When she was done, he got up and walked back to the booth.

"Sit," Max said, and he did, taking care to place himself in exactly the same spot as he had before. So maybe he wasn't as dumb as the grin and the pink shirt would lead one to believe. Which, of course, made it even more important to keep an eye on him. "You claim to know who I am. If that's true, then you must also know that I have to be careful."

"Yeah, sure."

"Maybe you're somebody with a grudge. Hell, maybe you're even a cop."

The eyes were amused. "Me? The heat? No, sir." He seemed to gain confidence. "Just a fan, that's all I am."

"A fan?" That was a new one to Max. He shook his head. "So who do you belong to, Jeremiah?"

He looked puzzled briefly, then shrugged. "Mostly I freelance. Nothing big, I gotta admit. Some numbers. Hot cars. Used to be an errand boy for Raphael Tadzio when I lived in Jersey."

"I know Tadzio."

"Yeah, everyone does."

"So you're into cars and numbers? That's it?"

"Mostly," he said, hedging. "Of course, I'm looking to better myself."

"Of course." Max lifted his beer again. "So. You want an autograph or what?"

It was midnight, almost an hour later than when he usually left the Swan. Max, after the glance at his watch, downed the rest of his final beer and stood.

Donahue looked over at the wall clock. "Yeah," he said with seeming reluctance. "It's about that time I guess, isn't it?"

"It is for me," Max said, dropping a bill onto the table. "A man my age needs his sleep."

"Sure," Donahue said scornfully. "You look like you're in pretty fine shape to me." He stood as well. "I might as well walk along with you."

"Are we going the same way?"

Donahue, pretending to be busy hunting change for a tip, didn't say anything.

Max shrugged and led the way out of the bar.

The sidewalk was still fairly crowded with late-night fun-seekers. It was a noisy, but seemingly good-natured, bunch. Max lighted a cigarette as they made their way slowly through the throng. "Used to be," he reminisced, "you could throw a bowling ball down this street at night and not hit anybody."

"Guess that's what they call progress."

"Maybe, maybe."

Max was still trying to get a good fix on this young man. They had spent almost three hours in the bar, drinking beer and talking—which, God knew, Donahue seemed able to do nonstop—but Max still didn't feel as if he had learned much.

Which meant one of two things: Either there wasn't much to learn, beyond what he saw; or else Donahue was real good at hiding whatever it was he wanted to hide. Max was pretty sure that the latter was the case. During the evening they'd exchanged views on the unseasonably warm weather, baseball, politics, and other subjects of even less importance. Only one thing was for certain: Donahue had a fast, smart mouth.

They paused at the fringe of a group gathered to watch a street musician. The boy was playing old Beatles songs on a cheap guitar. Donahue and a pretty black girl in the crowd improvised a few dance steps, and the audience responded with a few cheers and some hisses. The girl giggled, and Donahue took a bow.

Max shook his head and walked on. Donahue hurried to catch up. Apparently unable to simply proceed up the street in a normal fashion, he grabbed a light pole and swung around it, landing lightly in front of Max. "Can I ask you something, sir?"

"Stop calling me that."

"Okay. Uh, Max?" he said tentatively. "But can I ask?"

"I probably won't answer, but if it makes you happy, ask."

"I was just wondering what you're doing these days."

"Meaning?"

"Are you working?"

"I'm retired."

The look he got was skeptical and maybe a little puzzled. "Really? Max Trueblood is out of the business?"

Max took a final drag on the cigarette, then tossed the butt into the gutter. "Why the hell do you care?"

Four boys in sleeveless tees and headbands came toward them, between them, and it was a moment before they were side by side again.

"I'm just curious is all."

Max looked at him. "You're no virgin, Jeremiah, but what you might be is stupid. I'm going to do you a favor. Give you a little free advice."

"Okay."

"Never be curious. Curiosity can be a very unhealthy thing. Do you think that you can remember that?"

For a change Donahue didn't say anything. He didn't even smile, thank God. He just nodded.

Max stopped in front of his building. "This is as far as I go, kiddo. So long. And because I'm in a good mood, a little more advice. Still for free."

"What's that?"

"You ought to try to get a little smart."

Now Donahue smiled. "I'll try, Max. Thanks."

He climbed the steps, aware of the watching figure still below, and unlocked the door. Without looking down, Max went inside.

As he walked into the loft he hit the wall switch, washing the area in white light. Automatically, his gaze swept the area. No unexpected visitors this time. So maybe the two turkeys from the day before had been just a fluke. And maybe tonight was nothing more than what it had seemed to be. Maybe. Still . . .

He walked to the front window and parted the blinds just a little.

Donahue was still standing on the sidewalk below. He was smoking a cigarette and pacing in a tight circle near the curb. Occasionally, he would glance upward.

Max stayed where he was, watching, more sure than ever that there was more to Donahue than met even his practiced eye.

When the cigarette was gone, Donahue started trying to wave down a cab. It took several minutes and he ended up in a gypsy. The car was quickly lost from sight, and Max let the slats of the blind fall back into place.

Thoughtful, he walked into the kitchen and poured a glass of milk. Taking that and two Oreo cookies, he went to sit on the bed. He put the glass down and reached for the phone.

It took three calls for him to track down the man he was looking for. "Angie, this is Max."

"Long time no hear from, Max."

"Well, I don't need to know so much anymore."

"Ain't retirement grand?"

"It has its moments," Max said.

Someone spoke in the background and Angie's voice turned brisk. "What can I do for you, Max?"

"Is there something going on in the city? Something big?"

"Why do you ask? As a man no longer concerned."

"Call it curiosity." Max grimaced, remembering his warning to Donahue on that very subject just minutes before.

Angie was quiet briefly. "Well, there have been a couple of unfortunate accidents lately. Three, actually."

"What kind of accidents?"

"The kind where somebody steps in front of a bullet or two."

Max swallowed half a cookie. "That's too bad. Those unlucky victims—how high did they go in the overall scheme of things?"

"Not high. They were all just your basic foot soldier. Ain't they always the first to go?"

"The first, yes. But not usually the last. What's behind it?"

"That's all pretty murky at this point. I can tell you that a lot of people, even some very important people, are getting nervous." Angie was getting impatient. When a man had one of the biggest strings of teenaged hookers, female and male, in the city, it took a lot of time to keep things running smoothly. "Gotta run, Max. Why don't you just go sit on a beach someplace?" He hung up.

More slowly Max replaced the receiver. He picked up the glass and sipped milk carefully. All in all, it was a funny kind of situation. Pretty funny.

Of course, maybe it would all just blow over.

That could happen.

He hoped so. At least, he thought he hoped so. The really funny thing was, he couldn't be absolutely sure about that.

Jeremiah didn't think that being in Central Park at one in the morning was such a terrific idea. In fact, he thought it really sucked. But then, he wasn't there by choice. Not his choice, anyway. He was only following orders.

Stupid orders.

Even the cabdriver thought it was a stupid place to be. He just shook his head and said something in Spanish when Jeremiah told him to stop. Jeremiah could only catch a few of the words, but they seemed to insinuate, scornfully, that he was there looking for sex. Weird sex.

When the cab was gone, Jeremiah hunched his shoulders and walked over to the nearest bench, wishing he had the gun, which was resting safely in the drawer at home. It hadn't seemed like a smart idea to wear it and maybe give Trueblood ideas, but now he missed it.

Not far away, a group of dark shapes loomed. They were passing around a joint, of course. Sometimes Jeremiah had the idea that he was the only man in the whole fucking city who wasn't stoned. Well, him and probably Trueblood.

Definitely Trueblood.

He sat at the far end of the bench, as far from the shapes as he could. Damn, this was just crazy. What was wrong with the telephone, for chrissake?

After some nervous thought it occurred to him that maybe this meet, in this place, was part of the test. Like maybe to see whether or not he really had the balls to do the job.

He straightened his shoulders. Well, they would find out that Jeremiah Donahue had whatever it would take.

Still, there was no denying that he was very glad when a dark Lincoln slowed to a stop and a man emerged from the backseat. Two others climbed out of the front, but they stayed by the car, arms crossed, their eyes on the group nearby.

The first man walked over to the bench. "Donahue?" he said.

"Who the fuck else would be sitting here in the fucking middle of the night?" Jeremiah replied, having decided that maybe a little surly was the way to play it. No sense in letting them think he was some kind of damned puppy dog groveling for their approval.

"What's the matter, sweetheart? You up past your bed-time?" The voice, while mocking, was only vaguely inter-ested.

"I can think of better places to be right now than here."

"Indeed."

Indeed? Who the hell talked like that?

He was tall and very thin, dressed in a black suit. His appearance made Jeremiah think of that guy in the story about the headless horseman—what was his name? Ichabod Crane. Yeah, that was it. Wonderful. Here he was in the middle of Mugging Park, at God knew what time, with Ichabod Crane.

Maybe he was stoned, after all.

"So, Donahue, what do you have to tell me?"

"Not much yet, for chrissake. I met the guy at the bar, just like Mr. Tadzio suggested. We talked."

"And?" Ichabod examined his fingernails.

"And nothing, dammit. What do you expect? You people told me to take it easy, don't get him suspicious. He's no dummy."

"True. But you did at least manage to strike up an acquaintance?"

"I just said that, didn't I? We had some beers and talked."

"Good. Very good, in fact. Mr. Trueblood is not known for his amiability." Old Ichabod brushed at an invisible thread on the sleeve of his jacket.

"Lemme ask you a question."

"What?"

Jeremiah glanced over at the smokers; they seemed oblivious to him and the car. "If you want me to ice this guy, why don't I just wire his car and do it? Why all these games?"

Ichabod shook his head, apparently dismayed by the question. "Games, Jerry? Is that what you think we're doing here?" He shook his head again. "The elimination of Trueblood is just one part of a much larger picture. Everything has to happen at just the right time. We have information of certain things that are about to happen. And if they do—when they do—we need to be ready to respond. Understand?"

He didn't, really; but he nodded, anyway. "Okay. But what I really want to know is, how come him? He's just an old man—retired, even. So how come him?"

The man stood, looking down at him with eyes that seemed to glow almost yellow in the light. "Your job, Donahue, is not to ask so many questions. Or to wonder about our reasons. You have been employed to do just what you are told to do, when you are told to do it. Nothing more and nothing less. Do I make myself clear?"

"Entirely."

"Very good. I will pass on to Mr. Tadzio what you've told me. Meanwhile, keep on as you have been instructed."

"Yeah, sure. Why not?"

As he turned to go back to the car the man gave him what was probably intended to be a smile. "And if you're smart, Jerry, you won't linger here too long. The park can be a dangerous place to be at night." With that bit of wisdom he was gone.

"Thank you and fuck you," Jeremiah muttered to the disappearing headlights of the Lincoln.

Then he got up from the bench and walked away quickly.

At home, with the door safely closed between him and the rest of the city, Jeremiah wanted music. He wanted it good and loud, and the neighbors be damned. He selected some albums, stacked them on the turntable, and jacked up the volume. The first sounds blasted out, and he quickly turned the volume down to a more reasonable level. No sense making trouble.

As "Surfin' U.S.A." played, he took a beer and his gun out onto the fire escape. He held the weapon in one hand, trying to get comfortable with the feel as he pretended to shoot out the streetlights.

He didn't know that Sandy was above him until she spoke. "Hi."

"Whattcha say, babe?"

She didn't move from her perch on the sill. "Henry laid into me again." Her voice sounded funny, as if her lips were swollen, which they probably were. Henry was her pimp.

"You okay?"

"Oh, yeah." She laughed a little. "He ain't gonna do nothing that would mess me up for good. That would be bad business. He just likes to teach his girls a little lesson every so often."

"And what was the lesson this week?"

"You know what's funny? I can't even remember."

The Chiffons started in on "He's So Fine."

Jeremiah tracked a passing car with the gun. "You should probably do something about your life, Sandy."

"Yeah, probably. But there are days when I think I already am. I mean, you might not believe it, but this is the best place I've ever lived in. And it's the first time in my life that I've got more than one pair of shoes at a time."

"Well, that's great, I guess. But look at the price."

"We all gotta pay, Jerry. And the price is usually high."

He rubbed the barrel of the gun thoughtfully. She had a point. But he didn't say anything out loud.

"How's the new job going?"

"Fine. Okay, I guess." He gulped some beer, realizing as he swallowed it that the taste had gone suddenly sour, and he didn't want any more. He threw the can over the railing, watching as it hit the edge of the trash bin, then fell in. "Two points," he said.

"So what are you doing? In the job?"

"Not much so far. Learning the ropes, mostly. Talking to people."

"Well, you're sure good at that."

"Yeah, I am." He thought about what the skinny creep had said about Trueblood not being amiable. If that was supposed to mean like friendly, then the guy was wrong.

"Hey, Jerry, you want I should come down?"

He considered that, but then shook his head. "Not tonight. I'm really beat. And tomorrow might be a real long day. Think I'll just crash."

" 'Night, then."

He told her good night, then crawled back inside. After putting the gun away carefully, he undressed and got into bed. He hadn't been lying to her. All of a sudden he was more tired than he could remember ever being in his life.

And he was nervous.

Nervous, hell. He was scared.

But that was probably only normal, he told himself. Fear was a part of the price. Like Sandy getting the shit beat out of her every once in a while. It hurt, but she wanted the new shoes and a regular fix, so she took the beatings. She paid. He wanted to make something of his life, something better than what he had. And, for better or worse, this was the only way he knew to do that.

And if there was anybody who should be able to understand that simple fact, it would have to be Max Trueblood.

ONLY A JOB

one:

one step forward,
two steps back

1

Max was still working on the front page of the *Times* when his
door bell rang the next morning. For somebody who usually
never had company he was suddenly getting pretty damned
popular. He dropped the paper onto the counter and tight-
ened the belt of his robe before walking over to see who it
was.

There was a gun in the pocket of his robe, and he put one
hand on it as he opened the door.

"Mr. Trueblood?" The man standing there was too slick by
half. Not charming-slick like the con artist of the night before
but oily-slick. Like a door-to-door salesman or a lawyer.

As unpleasant as that might be, however, unless all
standards in his trade had fallen by the wayside, this creep
was not likely to pull a Smith & Wesson from the vest pocket
of his three-piecer and start blasting.

But Max kept his hand right where it was for the moment.
"I'm Trueblood. Who are you?"

"My name is David Hayes. I know it's early"—his cool aqua
gaze swept over Max's robe and bare feet; it wasn't actually all
that early—"but I wonder if we might talk?"

"Talk about what?"

Hayes obviously wasn't used to being kept on the outside of doors. He glanced around, then down to the sidewalk below. "If I might come in?" When Max didn't say anything he sighed. "I'm here on behalf of Mr. Marberg."

After another moment Max stepped to one side and let Hayes in. He was carrying a soft tan briefcase that must have cost a fortune and looked too thin to be holding even a single sheet of paper. Still, it was great for his image and it matched the suit. Max wondered if Hayes had a different case to go with every outfit.

It also occurred to him that he was meeting a lot of interesting people lately.

Hayes dropped the case onto the dining table and sat down. Max went on into the kitchen. "I was about to make my breakfast," he said. The remark was neither an apology nor a request for permission to continue. He took some eggs and cheese from the refrigerator. "Marberg already sent some message boys. I thought I made myself clear to them. So why did he send another one?"

Hayes's thin lips got even thinner. "I am not a 'message boy.' I am Mr. Marberg's executive assistant."

"Congratulations," Max said dryly. "Hard to tell the difference between this bunch and IBM these days, isn't it?"

"Business is business," Hayes said.

"Uh-huh." Max took the Jamaica Blue Mountain coffee beans from the cupboard and poured some into the grinder. For a moment the sound of the grinding process filled the room. Then he said, "I don't have anything to tell you that I didn't already say to the two assholes who were already here."

Hayes looked a little embarrassed. "First of all, let me say that Mr. Marberg sincerely regrets what happened earlier. Apparently there was some kind of breakdown in communications."

"Apparently there was. Sending a couple of apes like that into my home. To 'get' me, they said." Max slammed a small omelet pan onto the stove. "That shows no respect, Mr. Executive Assistant. I am Max Trueblood, not some cheap triggerman."

"We apologize. What else can I say? Mistakes happen."

"Fine, you apologize." He smeared some butter into the pan. "We accept. It's nice to see that good manners are not altogether dead, even in this city. But that doesn't change the basic fact."

"What basic fact is that?"

"That I'm retired, just like I told Heckle and Jeckle."

"We know that."

"So why are you here?"

"To issue an invitation."

Max broke three eggs into a bowl. "An invitation?"

"Mr. Marberg would like you to come to lunch today."

"He would?" Max stirred the eggs. "I know Sam Marberg a long time. I knew his father a little, even—before the old man died. We never had lunch before."

Hayes assumed what was probably supposed to be his leveling-with-you look. It made him seem even more like a snake-oil salesman. "Max, I won't try to bullshit you. We respect you too much for that, okay?"

Max smiled vaguely.

"The truth is, Mr. Marberg wants to talk to you. He has a deal. A very good job. What would it hurt to come see him, have a little wine, some lunch? Talk about the offer, anyway. What do you say?"

Max thought it over as he poured the egg and cheese mixture into the hot pan. Finally he nodded. "All right. Lunch. But that doesn't mean I'm interested in whatever deal he's pushing. You got that clear?"

"I understand. Mr. Marberg will be very pleased. About two, if that's acceptable?"

"Fine."

Hayes picked up his briefcase and left.

Max locked the door, then started making some toast. He hoped this all wasn't a real big mistake.

Several hours later, as he was starting to get ready for the unexpected and vaguely troubling lunch, Max was still hoping that he was doing the right thing. But sometimes a man had very little choice. This seemed like one of those times. Too much was going on, and it would be stupid just to sit back on his ass and hope that it would all blow over.

It wasn't going to disappear, which meant that out of self-preservation, if nothing else, he'd better get a handle on the situation. Lunch with Marberg seemed as good a place as any to start.

Max wanted to be sure that Marberg knew that just because he'd been out of circulation for a while, he hadn't lost any of his edge. That meant he had to look good. He put on some freshly pressed khaki pants with a white shirt and a pale lilac tie. He liked the tie, which he'd bought on impulse one day while walking through Bloomingdale's.

Instead of the tiny ankle gun he donned his shoulder holster and put the Magnum into it. Not that he expected to have any call at all to use the thing—Marberg wasn't that stupid—but he had to go into this meet like a man ready for anything. Otherwise Marberg would lose respect for him.

Even for someone who had retired, that would not be a good thing.

Just before leaving the apartment, Max put on a white linen sportcoat and his favorite soft canvas hat. Nobody could say he'd allowed himself to slip.

It was still another warm, sunny day, and the city seemed to have forgotten that it was actually September and that fall had to be lurking somewhere just around the next corner. Max took his sunglasses out of his jacket pocket and put them on.

Max probably should have been surprised to find one Jeremiah Donahue standing in front of the gallery. Maybe he should have been, but he wasn't. What did surprise him, at

least a little, was that he didn't mind very much. Donahue
amused him. He walked over. "Hello, Jeremiah," he said.

"Hiya, Max." Donahue gestured toward the display of
Polish religious wood carvings currently on display in the
window of the gallery. "That stuff expensive?"

"For you, yes. Prohibitively, I imagine."

Donahue shrugged philosophically.

"What are you doing here, anyway?"

"Well, I was just in the neighborhood," he said. "Thought
maybe we could do something. Like get lunch?"

Max looked at him for a moment. There was no guile
apparent. Just a lean young man in a pair of jeans that had
been cut off short and a Jets T-shirt. Hard to hide deception in
those so-friendly blue eyes, and harder still to hide a gun in
those clothes. "You were in the neighborhood? That's flimsy,
kiddo, very flimsy."

Donahue just shrugged again.

"Walk with me," Max said. It was only slightly more than a
suggestion.

Jeremiah fell into step cheerfully. "Where are we going?"

"Lunch," Max said. Just that one word.

"Okay."

"You're a very agreeable young man, Jeremiah. So agreeable, in fact, that I can't help but wonder a little bit."

Jeremiah neatly sidestepped a speeding skateboard propelled by a girl with flowing golden hair. "Wonder about
what?"

"About you. About maybe you're after something. Are
you?"

Jeremiah glanced at him, squinting a little against the sun.
"Hey, Max, isn't everybody after something? In one way or
another?"

It was so blatantly honest, so calculatedly disarming, that it
made Max wonder all the more.

And he wondered about something else too. If Jeremiah
was right about everybody being after something, then maybe

the real question was not what Donahue was after but what he, Max Trueblood, was looking for.

Maybe the answer to that was simple as a few laughs. Donahue could do that, make him laugh. But that wasn't good enough, not by a long shot.

Okay: For sure, Sam Marberg wouldn't like the idea of an unexpected lunch guest. Getting a chance to aggravate the bastards at the top was always nice. So probably that was part of the reason he was suddenly doing things that shouldn't be done.

Better, but still a little weak.

Well, it shouldn't be forgotten that Donahue was still basically an unknown factor in this whole thing. Probably the best way to find out just what the hell he was up to was to keep a close eye on him. Take him to lunch, for example. When you were keeping tabs on a man, he was less likely to pull any kind of surprise. Like blowing your fool head off.

Now that made sense. It satisfied Max.

He stopped trying to find justifications for his actions. To dig any deeper might uncover things that he'd rather not think about. Like boredom and maybe even loneliness. Which made no sense at all.

Max shook his head. Christ. Between whatever the hell was going on with Marberg and whatever Donahue was up to, Max was getting tired. Maybe he should have taken Angie's advice and found a quiet beach someplace.

Instead he waved for a cab.

When the taxi stopped, they got out in front of a Gramercy Park brownstone. Jeremiah looked from Max to the heavy oak door and the man sitting on the stoop, doing what was obviously guard duty. The skinny redhead had been demoted.

"I thought we were just going to have some lunch," Jeremiah said, a new note of hesitancy in his voice.

Max finished paying the driver. "We are. With Sam Marberg."

"*The* Sam Marberg?"

"You do get around, don't you, Jeremiah? You know Marberg, then?"

"Just by name, of course." He eyed the guard again, but Red was pretending not to notice them. "Why are we having lunch with him?"

"Because he asked me nice. And you wanted to have lunch, didn't you?"

Jeremiah tugged at the edge of his T-shirt. "Hell, I'm not dressed for this kind of thing. I figured a hot dog from a cart, you know?"

"Let this be a lesson to you. A man should always be ready for anything." Max smiled, then spoke to Red as if they had never met before. "Trueblood. He's expecting me."

Red nodded and disappeared inside. A lot of the starch had gone out of his attitude. Max approved.

Jeremiah glanced around, an edge of desperation on his face. "Hey, Max, why don't you just go have lunch with him? I'll take off, and maybe we can catch up with each other later. Doesn't that sound like a good idea?" As he spoke, he was edging along the curb.

Max reached out and clamped one hand around the other man's arm. Donahue looked startled at the strength in the grip. "We're having lunch, Mr. Slick. Why, who knows, this could be a very smart career move for a bright lad like you. Marberg might have a spot just made for somebody with your talents."

Jeremiah opened his mouth again, as if to argue further, then, after another look at Max's face, he gave up. "What the fuck," he said. "Let's have lunch."

"Good boy," Max said.

The makeshift doorman returned and waved them into the house. As they stood in the front hall Max opened his jacket so that the gun he wore was clearly visible. "This stays with me," he said.

"Yeah, the boss said it was okay," Red mumbled.

Jeremiah raised his hands. "I got nothing," he said cheerfully.

That earned him a scornful glance. "Yeah," Red said. "Follow me."

"Talks up a real storm, doesn't he?" Jeremiah whispered as they headed down a long hallway.

"Keeping your mouth shut is sometimes a real good idea," Max replied pointedly.

The further things went, the more Max wondered why the hell he was doing this. Whatever "this" was. It certainly wasn't part of the agenda.

But it was fun.

Fun, for chrissake. That was the dumbest reason for doing anything.

Still, though, when a man was retired, wasn't he allowed to have a few good times just for a change? Of course, the trouble with thinking like that was that this kind of fun could end up getting him killed.

Oh, well, to quote a friend: What the fuck, let's have lunch.

They were shown into a vast living room furnished—overcrowded, in fact—with what appeared to be genuine antiques. Max thought that it looked more like a museum than a place where real people lived. There was such a thing as having taste, and there was such a thing as having money. In his opinion, if you had to have a lot of one and not much of the other, it should be all taste and little cash. This room was painful evidence of the reverse.

"Shit," came a whisper very close to his ear. "Little crimes might not pay, but the big ones sure as hell do, right?"

Max shot him a dirty look, then turned as Marberg entered the room. He was a stocky, dark man, wearing bright blue contact lenses and an Armani suit. Moving toward them, he extended a hand. Two rings glittered on the fingers. "Max, Max, it's been too long. How're you doing?" He sounded hearty.

"Fine, Sam," Max replied in a neutral tone. "Enjoying the quiet life."

"So I hear, so I hear." Abruptly, the cold, phony blue gaze settled on Donahue. "Who's this?"

"My bodyguard," Max said.

Donahue's mouth fell open, but for a change nothing came out.

Marberg only looked amused. "Your bodyguard? I wouldn't think that a man like you would need one. You never did before, and now that you're out of the business, it seems a waste."

"Yes, well, I never thought I needed one before, either. But in this day and age you never know, right? What with the crime rate soaring like it is. Hell, I came home just recently and found two scumbags in my living room. In broad daylight, even."

Marberg spread his hands, smiling. "Hayes told me that you two got that little misunderstanding all worked out."

"I guess."

Marberg offered drinks; apparently, he was determined to play the role of a congenial host. The whole thing was making Max distinctly cautious. Whatever the hell Marberg wanted, it had to be big. But there was nothing to do but wait until the dope decided to talk about it.

He asked for Scotch on the rocks, assuming that it would be quality stuff. Jeremiah, who was sitting on one corner of the overstuffed sofa, absently scuffing his right Puma back and forth in the deep carpet, chose the same.

Hayes joined them, helping himself to a glass of wine.

Conversation didn't rise above the insignificant during that round of drinks or the second. Just about the time that the room was beginning to close in claustrophobically on Max, Marberg rose and led the way into a dining room that was nearly as vast and every bit as overly furnished as the living room.

The master of the house paused in the doorway. "Used to

be three houses," he said. "I bought all three of them, and we knocked out the walls for space."

"Very nice," Max said.

A crime, he thought. Marberg should be arrested for that if nothing else.

Someone had apparently hustled into the room during the social hour and set a fourth place at the table. An immense crystal chandelier sparkled overhead.

Talk remained mundane as the four men ate pasta with lobster sauce, spinach salad, and then fresh strawberries in heavy cream. Jeremiah ate with enthusiasm but kept his comments to himself. That encouraged Max; maybe he was trainable.

Finally, the silent black waiter served coffee and left the room. That seemed to be the signal for things to get serious. "So, Max," Marberg said. "You're probably wondering about the reason for this lunch."

"Your errand boy here said you had a job to discuss. I agreed to do you the courtesy of coming to hear you out about it."

Hayes flushed angrily at the job description. Donahue snickered a little. Dumb move on his part, because then Hayes got mad at him, too, and Hayes didn't look like the kind of man to forget something like that.

Marberg chose to ignore the moment. "I appreciate you coming. And, yes, there is a job."

Max sipped the coffee. It was good; not great, but good. Hayes seemed to swallow his anger, at least for the moment. Jeremiah was occupied stirring sugar into his coffee.

"I'm retired," Max said.

"Yes, all right, dammit. Everybody knows that. But this is just a onetime deal. This is special."

"How special?"

Marberg hesitated, glancing at Donahue.

Jeremiah just looked bewildered.

Max smiled. "You can talk in front of him."

"You swear for Donahue?"

"For my bodyguard?" Max shrugged. "Of course." He didn't know whose expression was the more interesting, Marberg's or Jeremiah's.

After a moment Marberg accepted it. "This job is the kind of special that will pay you two hundred grand."

A sound came from the end of the table; it might have been a gasp, but nobody looked toward Donahue.

Max set his cup down carefully. "Sam, you know me better than that, don't you? When did I ever talk money first? You tell me the job and I set the fee."

Marberg looked down at the tabletop for a moment, as if he needed to rein in a burst of temper or impatience. When he looked up, he spoke quietly. "I want you to remove Nick Costa."

"Costa?" Max, showing nothing on his face or in his tone, turned the name over in his mind. "Hell, that man is better protected than the fucking president. Nobody ever even tried offing Costa before." He nodded slowly. "Yes, that would be a job worth two hundred grand. In fact, I think that's worth two hundred fifty. For whoever does the job."

"I want you on this, Max. You're still the best."

"I'm retired."

Marberg finally gave in to his frustration. "If you tell me that one more fucking time . . ." He glanced at Hayes, then took a deep breath. "Nobody is so goddamn comfortable that two hundred grand—oh, two hundred fifty thousand, then— wouldn't make it better."

"Maybe."

Smoothly, Hayes got to his feet. "Sam, why don't we leave Max for a few minutes? Let him think about it?"

"Good idea," Marberg said grudgingly. Both men headed for the door. "Help yourselves to cigars and brandy," Marberg said before leaving.

The room was quiet when they had gone.

Max stood and went to the sideboard. He poured snifters of

brandy and took a couple of cigars from the humidor. He walked back to the table and sat next to Donahue. They each tasted the brandy.

"So, Max, you gonna do it?"

"Bears thinking about, I guess. What do you think?"

"Me?" He looked uncomfortable. "Why ask me?"

"Better you than the wallpaper," Max said.

Jeremiah licked at his upper lip. "Well, it's a lot of money."

"True. Of course, I have enough money already."

"Lucky you."

"Luck had very little to do with it, actually." Max leaned back in the chair. "But just between you and me, Donahue, this retirement shit isn't all it's cracked up to be. Sometimes it gets a little boring."

Jeremiah seemed to find something funny. "Well, killing Nicholas Costa should pump a little excitement into your life."

Max smiled. "At the very least."

"So?"

Max snipped the end off one of the cigars and handed the stogie to him. "You serious about moving up in the business?"

"Serious? Yeah, sure. Yeah." Jeremiah absently snapped the expensive cigar in two.

Max shook his head. "So I suppose we could think of this little exercise as on-the-job training." He looked at his own cigar for a moment, then put it down. "Should I do it?"

"Am I supposed to decide this?" The words held an unexpected flash of anger.

"Live dangerously, Jeremiah."

There was a long silence. Finally, Jeremiah nodded. "Do it," he said harshly. "Do the fucking hit."

"Okay," Max heard himself say. "I will."

Why? For the money? He could only spend so much, and who the hell would he leave it to? To show this dumb jerk-off the fine art of killing? Hardly. Why the hell should he care if Donahue improved himself or not?

Just do the goddamn job, he told himself. Play this hand out and see what happens.

Maybe it would all go down just the way it should, the way it always had before. In which case he'd be some dough ahead and a lot less bored. Or it could go wrong and he'd end up dead, which would also mean that he wouldn't be bored.

He shook his head, disgusted. Christ, he was turning into a crazy old man. Pretty soon he'd be picking through trash cans.

Jeremiah picked up his snifter and drained it in one gulp. "So you're really gonna do it?"

"That's a helluva way to treat fine cognac. You don't gulp this stuff, dummy, you sip it." Max sipped his own drink, then set it down again. "We're going to do it. You and me."

"You and me?" Jeremiah picked up Max's glass and took a small sip. "Why me?"

"Why not?"

"Is that an answer?"

"All I got. Besides, you're asking the wrong question."

"Oh?"

"I already said that I'm going to do it. The real question is, are you in with me?"

Jeremiah chewed on his lip for a second, then nodded. "Yeah. Sure. Sure, I am." He looked at Max. "How much are you going to pay me?"

"Pay you?" Max reached over and took back the snifter. He drank. "Why the hell should I pay you anything? Maybe you should pay me. After all, you have a great opportunity here. A chance to learn from a master. That should be enough, unless you're greedy."

"But if I'm going to help, don't I deserve a cut? And, hell, you keep saying how you don't need the fucking money, anyway. I can hardly pay my rent, if you want the truth."

Max considered it for a moment. "Okay," he said. "I'll pay you."

Jeremiah brightened. "How much?"

Max smiled. "Whatever I think you're worth."

The door opened, and Marberg came back into the room. Max stood. "Okay, Sam. Two hundred fifty grand. Standard terms: half now and the rest deposited in the usual manner."

"I knew we could count on you, Max."

Hayes came in then, carrying a plain brown briefcase. It didn't match his suit, but then it probably didn't belong to him. He opened the case and carefully counted out the proper amount. Max tried not to smile as he watched Donahue watch the money changing hands.

The remaining details were settled quickly, and in only a few minutes Max and Jeremiah were standing on the sidewalk. "So that takes care of that," Max said, putting on his hat.

"I guess it does."

"Nothing like starting at the top, kiddo."

Jeremiah glanced at him. "Yeah?"

"He wasn't exaggerating in there. I am the best."

"I believe it."

Max stopped walking. "See that car over there? The blue one?"

"Yeah."

"Cops."

Jeremiah froze. "The cops?"

"Sure. Probably watching Marberg's place. Or maybe watching me, though God knows why." He laughed. "You can breathe, Jeremiah. They're sure as hell not watching you."

"No, I guess not. Why would they?"

Max donned his sunglasses. "Call me tomorrow. Early."

"Call you?"

"Yeah." Max handed him a card with the number. "I've got things to do now." He started off. "Take it easy."

"You too."

Max kept moving, giving him a wave.

2

When the door opened and the two men came out of Marberg's house, Aaron was so surprised that he stopped playing with the unlit cigar. "I'll be goddamned," he said.

"What?" said a bored voice coming from the direction of the driver's seat. Staring at the bad guy's house for just less than two hours was not Cody Blaine's idea of having a good time.

"That's Max Trueblood."

"Who?"

Didn't they teach the young cops anything these days? Aaron sighed and pointed with the end of the cigar. "Max Trueblood. Best damned hitter in the business."

That, at least, caught his partner's interest, and he leaned forward over the steering wheel for a better look. "Which one?"

"Which one? Are you kidding or what? You seriously think that the boychik with the legs has at least a hundred kills behind him?"

"That old man, you mean? He's a triggerman?"

"He's a fucking artist is what Trueblood is. And he's not so old, partner. Max and I go back together, in fact."

"Trueblood?" Cody seemed to think about it for a moment. "Yeah, I guess the name does ring a bell."

"It should." Aaron watched the two men. "I just can't figure out what the hell he's doing here. Max retired last year."

Cody snickered. "They give him a party and a gold watch?"

"He didn't need a watch. I figure he's got a real nice little bank account. Better than a civil servant, that's for damned sure."

"What about the other one? The boychik?"

Aaron concentrated his gaze on the younger man. "Him, I don't know."

It was certainly interesting, anyway. Aaron was starting to get a strong feeling that something very big was happening. This might get real exciting before long. Max had never been boring, that was for damned sure, not in the forty or so years he had known him.

When both Trueblood and the stranger, going in opposite directions, were out of sight, Cody started the car. "I assume we can go now? If you've had your fill of staring at Sam Marberg's front door?"

"Okay, okay, we can go." Aaron began the process of lighting the cigar. "Max Trueblood," he murmured, more to himself than to Cody. "What the hell is that old bastard up to?"

Cody, who was probably thinking about lunch and who probably didn't think that a bad guy old enough to collect a pension was worth much worrying about, didn't answer.

As for Aaron, he could hardly wait to find out what was going to happen next.

Whatever happened, he wanted to be right on top of it, so Aaron broke one of his own rules—the one which called for as little contact as possible with the powers that be—and went in to see the captain.

Virgil Higgins had been a pretty good cop when he was out in the trenches. But he was a better politician and he was also black. That combination put him on a fast track, back in the more radical days of the immediate past, and he rose to the captaincy.

Aaron got along with him but no more than that. They exchanged a little polite chatter when the meeting began, then Aaron got down to his purpose in being there. "I think something big is about to blow up in the local family scene," he said.

Higgins was eating gumdrops to keep from smoking. Never

a small man, this new vice had already added about fifteen pounds to his frame. He chewed thoughtfully before answering. "I haven't heard anything."

Aaron did not comment that way up here where Higgins stayed it was hard to hear the rumbles in the street. "Three killings," he said. "And I've picked up some other indications."

"Uh-huh." Higgins debated a choice of red or green gumdrop. He took the green. "Well, you're the expert." He smiled. "Of course, maybe you just want a little heavy action before your exit, right?"

Aaron didn't respond to that.

Higgins nodded. "Okay, Aaron, what do you want?"

"I want to be kept on top of whatever happens. If a radio car gets a killing that even looks like it might be mob-connected, I want immediate notification. Wherever it happens, whenever."

"You can't have any extra manpower. We're stretched too damn thin as it is."

"That's fine. My partner and I can handle it. Just give us the flexibility to move."

Higgins always considered things before making a decision. Aaron could never figure out if that meant he was really thoughtful or just not too bright. Finally, his face cleared and he picked up a yellow gumdrop. "Okay, Aaron. Maybe you can go out on a winning streak. Take your hunch and run with it."

Aaron nodded, took a purple gumdrop, and left.

There was some of the inevitable paperwork to keep them in the squad room longer than either man wanted to remain that evening. It was one of the things they were in complete agreement on, the hatred of typing and filing. Two hours of it put both Aaron and Cody into a foul mood.

By unspoken agreement they walked around the corner to the Off-Duty Bar and took their usual booth toward the back.

When Cody had fetched a beer for Aaron and a Coke for himself, he settled back and lit a cigarette. "So. Fill me in a little on this guy Trueblood."

Aaron had known that Cody would decide, eventually, to get interested. He tasted his beer first, then nodded. "Yeah. Max. You know, I've been watching that son of a bitch since, jesuschrist, 1945, when I was still on traffic detail. Can you believe that?"

"You never busted him?"

"Never even gave him a fucking parking ticket. And I tried. God, I tried. But the man is beautiful. He makes a hit and it's squeaky clean. I mean, perfect. I know the bastard's a killer, but me knowing it doesn't mean shit."

"Has he really made a hundred hits?"

"At least. That's just a minimum. Hell, it could be twice that. Maybe he's killed a thousand, I don't know. I'll ask him someday."

"Oh, sure. What'll you do, just walk up to him and say, 'Mr. Trueblood, sir, excuse me, but how many people have you iced during your illustrious career?'"

"Max would just laugh. Hell, knowing him, he might even tell me. Knowing that I couldn't prove a damn thing." Aaron contemplated the bubbles in his beer for a moment. "I've spent a lot of time over the years trying to figure that man out."

"What's to figure?" Cody said. "He's a killer, like you said. Just another punk in a city full of them."

"Punk? Nah, that word doesn't apply here." He shrugged. "Hell, I don't know. Wait until you meet him, then you'll see what I mean."

"Well, gosh, that's a pleasure I'm looking forward to with bated breath."

Sometimes Cody could be irritatingly sarcastic.

He swallowed some Coke and noisily crunched the ice between his molars. "Anyway, if he's retired like you said, then what's he doing visiting Marberg?"

"That's the question."

"Social call, maybe?"

Aaron shook his head. "I doubt it. Max worked for the bosses, but I don't think he ever liked them much. He's not a very sociable guy."

"So . . . what, then?"

"That's what I'd like to know. Like you said, he's old. Out of the picture."

"But you said he's your age. And you're not out of the picture."

"Soon, partner, soon." But Aaron pushed that thought aside. Wanting to change the subject and casting around for a topic, he asked, "How's . . . Amanda?" He couldn't quite get used to the fact of cops actually living with girls they weren't married to, but that seemed to be the way of it these days, so he adjusted. You had to adjust or you'd get left behind. Maybe, given the times, he should just be glad that it was a girl his partner was shacking up with. Cody, at any rate, seemed not to care about either the legality or the morality of it, since he talked about the girl a lot. Or he used to, anyway, but not so much anymore, which was why Aaron had asked.

"She's okay." Cody bent the plastic straw he wasn't using. "Bitching about my hours, mostly."

"They will do that. Women."

"I try to explain, but . . ." He shrugged.

"Yeah." Aaron didn't really feel up to advising him on this. After all, when his wife walked out all those years ago, she didn't even bother to leave him a note. It wasn't really necessary, of course, because he knew exactly why she was going. They'd been arguing about all of the reasons for a long time.

"Oh, well," Cody said philosophically. That seemed to end the conversation.

Cody could hear the taped sitar music even before he opened the door. That was a bad sign. Mandy only played that stuff when she was having one of her moods. Eastern thought didn't always mesh well with trying to understand the psyche of a New York City homicide cop.

He already knew what the evening ahead would hold: Brown rice for dinner and another debate on the shaky morality of his job.

Morality?

He wasn't even sure what the word meant anymore.

Cody sighed wearily and opened the door.

Mandy was sitting on the floor, in the damn lotus position, her eyes closed as she listened to the music. He closed the door quietly so that nobody could possibly blame him for bringing disruptive auras into the apartment.

He stood in the foyer, taking off the holster and watching her. God, but she was beautiful. She always reminded him of Farrah Fawcett when she used to play on *Charlie's Angels*. Silky blonde hair fell around her face in soft waves, and the white jumpsuit she was wearing fit her body in a way that managed to be both sexy and innocent at the same time.

Cody hung the gun on the doorknob.

She opened her eyes. "Hi."

"Hi." He sat next to her, legs crossed Indian-style.

"You're late."

"Not very."

"Late enough. We were going to see that movie tonight."

He'd forgotten. "I'm sorry." And he was, sort of, but in a way he was also glad to miss it. She liked all those foreign films, the kind with subtitles, and that was too much like work.

She got up smoothly and started to put the meal on the table. "Never mind. Maybe I'll hit the matinee tomorrow."

Cody stood as well and went to pour himself some orange juice. "Who with?"

"Why does it have to be with anybody?"

It didn't, of course, but he knew that it would be. She knew a lot of people from her work in the museum. Artists and like that. Sensitive types who liked movies nobody but they could understand and who thought that anybody who carried a .44 Magnum around every day was a Fascist.

Still, he was busy, and there was no reason why she shouldn't go places and do things with her friends.

She set a clay bowl of rice on the table.

Cody wondered how much longer they could last. Maybe he could try a little harder and save it. But not right now. This whole thing with the mob killings, and now Max Trueblood, was just starting to heat up. Once it was out of the way, maybe Mandy and he could manage a few days off, take a trip, and work everything out.

If only she would serve him a steak once in a while. Hell, even the goddamn rice would taste better with a good sirloin.

3

Aaron sat at the kitchen table and went through the mail as a Swanson's turkey dinner defrosted and heated in the oven. There were some bills, which he set aside until the end of the month, and some ads that he pitched immediately. The only other item was an envelope postmarked Westchester. He had a beer before opening that one.

The note from his daughter asked him to have dinner in the city. He decided to accept and make it the occasion for a little truth-telling. Also included in the envelope was a crayon drawing. Aaron studied it briefly, trying to decide whether it was a green elephant or a misshapen tree. Then he tossed both the note and the drawing into the wastebasket.

He sat at the table for a few more minutes as the smell of turkey and aluminum filled the kitchen.

Traffic was light going back into Manhattan, and he made good time. It wasn't until he actually parked in front of the apartment building and flipped the official business sign into place that Aaron realized maybe he should have called first.

But it was too late now, so he just locked the car and went on into the building.

The doorman, who was new since his last visit, asked his name and then called upstairs. "You may go right on up, sir," he said after the brief call. Something in the tone led Aaron to think that he didn't quite measure up to the usual quality of visitor here. But after being a cop for so long, Aaron was used to that. A policeman never really fit in anywhere, except with others of his ilk.

The elevator was quiet. Nice to ride in one that didn't have the damned music assaulting your ears. He reached the fifteenth floor and walked to the end of the hall. As he arrived, the door opened.

Pamela St. Germaine was as lovely as ever, although Aaron knew damned well that she had to be pushing sixty. The long satin thing she was wearing, not a dress and not quite a robe either, was champagne-colored, matching her hair. She smiled and let him in. "Aaron, it's been a long time."

He felt suddenly awkward. "I apologize for just showing up like this. Should have called."

But she waved off his apology, ushering him into the living room, then bringing brandy and two glasses. "An old friend like you doesn't need an invitation."

Pamela, who had started life as Hilda Bosch, began her career as a very young streetwalker, which was what they were called in those days. She was arrested only once, by a young rookie named Aaron Temple. That was worth a fine, which she paid almost cheerfully. Soon after that she caught the attention of one of the city's most powerful politicians and her career was made. From street-corner whore to high-class call girl, and finally to a role as the madam of her own house, a ritzy joint that catered to only the top names in the city and was never raided once. Not even during the periodic crackdowns on vice in the Big Apple. When Pamela finally left the business, it was as a very rich woman.

Aaron considered her a friend.

Over the years they had passed through many stages in their relationship, from mutual antipathy to sneaking fondness and into a sort of passion that finally evolved into affection.

He leaned back, watching as she poured the brandy. "You look good, Pamela," he said.

"Thank you, sir." She handed him a glass. "You look a little tired."

"Ahh, well." Aaron knew damned well what he looked like: a white-haired, thin man who limped, wore old-fashioned wire-framed glasses, and dressed in cheap suits off the rack. "The job, you know."

"You've been complaining about the job forever." They toasted one another silently, and Pamela smiled. "You hate to think about leaving it, don't you?"

"God, yes."

He got up from the sofa and wandered over to the window. "Do you ever get tired of this view?" he asked, staring at the lights of Central Park below.

"Never. And you're changing the subject."

He shrugged.

"How's that partner of yours working out?"

"Fine. Blaine's a good kid. Eager. We might be on the verge of something big." His voice dwindled off as he thought about it. Then he turned around and looked at her again. "Did you ever meet a man named Max Trueblood?" The question, he knew, came very close to violating the silent terms of their friendship. But they were all so old now, him and Pamela and Max. What could it matter?

She was quiet, her tongue playing around the rim of the snifter. "I think so. Yes, years ago. I seem to remember the name. Why?"

Indeed, why? What possible relevance could this information have to what was happening now? "No reason, I guess," he said lamely. "I was just curious."

"It's funny, isn't it?"

"What's that?"

"It sometimes seems to me that life is like a circle. We all go around and around in the same place."

He wasn't quite sure what she meant, but he didn't say that. Instead he walked back over and sat down again. "I never had supper," he said. "We could go get something."

But she said no, that she'd whip something up. They each had another brandy, then went into the kitchen. She made soup and sandwiches with some kind of white cheese that he'd never had before. It was all very good.

When the food was gone and the last of the coffee finished, a brief silence fell over them. Aaron lit his third cigar of the day.

Pamela got up and turned off the overhead light, leaving the room in a dim glow. "Would you like to stay, Aaron?" she asked.

He thought for a moment. "For a while," he said.

He wondered if her bedroom still smelled of violets, the way it always had.

two:

file that under
"who gives a damn"

1

His was the only white face in Ernie's Bar-B-Que Heaven. It always was. In fact, he probably could have traveled blocks in any direction from here without seeing another one. Max didn't really understand why—Ernie served up the best damned ribs in the world, and in the twenty-five years he'd been coming here nothing bad had happened.

He sat at his regular table, drinking a Pabst and eyeing the chalkboard that was the only menu. The bill of fare never changed, but he always read it, anyway.

The young girl waiting tables—the latest in a long line of pretty kids in tight pants that Ernie employed—finally wandered over. The girls were never hired for either their brains or their ambition, so service here tended toward the erratic. Nobody seemed to mind very much. This girl was so new to the job that she obviously was surprised to see him. But she didn't ask why a white guy was in here. She just cheerfully popped her gum and waited.

Max took his time, as if there were some real decision to make, although he always ordered the same thing. "Back ribs. Corn. Double order of cole slaw. Bread and butter."

She wrote all of that down in a painfully slow hand. "How you want them ribs?" she asked in a breathy whisper.

Ernie made them four ways—mild, spicy, extra spicy, and incendiary. Max ordered them incendiary, knowing he'd regret it in the middle of the night but unable to resist. What was life worth unless a man was willing to take a few chances along the way? Which reminded him that he hadn't collected from Buggy yet; the filly, Take A Chance, had turned up a winner. Maybe that was a good sign.

At least his culinary courage raised him in the girl's estimation, because she grinned and popped the gum twice.

"And another beer," Max added.

She nodded and turned away.

"And, sweetheart, tell Ernie that I'd like to talk to him, would you, please?"

At that she looked a little skeptical, but then she just nodded again and disappeared through the swinging doors that led to the kitchen.

Although he would have come all the way up here just for the ribs, Max usually didn't. Most often he had a dual purpose for a visit. Ernie, a massive former Alabamian who loved food, football, and young girls, not necessarily in that order, had a talent. While he never seemed to leave the kitchen, he had somehow developed a terrific pipeline of information about people. He seemed to have a little dope, or was able to dig up a little dope, about almost any name you could toss out. "People," he liked to say, "are my hobby."

It was a hobby that also paid him rather nicely on occasion.

The food came quickly, and Max dug in with enthusiasm. This meal pleased him more than had the fancy lunch at Marberg's. He was about halfway through the platter before Ernie appeared, wiping his massive hands on a soiled apron.

"Maximilian," he said in a surprisingly soft voice. "Where the hell you been? I was beginning to think you up and died."

"Not yet. Although this sauce might do the trick tonight."

Ernie grinned and lowered his over three hundred pounds

into a chair. The chair creaked but held. "You looks like a man with something on his mind."

"Yeah. I've got a name and I wonder what you might be able to tell me about it."

Ernie just nodded.

"Guy named Jeremiah Donahue."

"And what do you want to know about this Mr. Donahue?"

"Whatever you can tell me."

"Gimme a few minutes." Ernie went back to his kitchen and his telephone.

Max picked up the second ear of corn and gnawed on it thoughtfully. Donahue was charming. Agreeable. Too much of both to be very believable. He was up to something for sure, and Max had a pretty good idea what that something was.

The question was, then, why waste time on him? And more urgently, why the hell drag him into the deal with Marberg?

Max tried, but he still couldn't come up with any answer that really satisfied him. If the meal itself didn't give him a massive dose of indigestion, thinking about this whole thing would.

He was sopping up the last of the deadly sauce with the final crust of bread by the time Ernie reappeared. "How much is this meal going to cost me, by the way?"

Ernie considered. "Oh, I think mebbe a hundred will cover it."

"Price of cabbage gone up, has it?"

"Ain't everything?"

"You have a point. So?"

Ernie took a toothpick out of his mouth. "Donahue, Jeremiah P. Born in Hoboken, if you can believe that."

"I can."

"His momma was a working girl. Father unknown. Could've been any of her tricks. The boy growed up on the streets, and Momma loved the needle, which killed her off early. Donahue's been a flunky for Raphael Tadzio since he was a kid. Still is, far as I know."

"He still works for Tadzio?"

"Seems like. Never nothing too big, not that I can prove, you see, but rumor has it that the young man is a real comer."

Max wiped a paper napkin across his mouth. "I can also believe that." He could tell that Ernie had more; he always had a canary-eating expression when he could pass along something really good. "So what else does the rumor mill say?"

"This is purely speculative, you understand?"

"Yeah, yeah, get to it."

"Some folks are of the opinion that the boy has a knack with things of an explosive nature. The name of one deceased Alphonse was mentioned, just by way of example."

Now, Max found that bit of information very interesting, even if it was only speculation. So Donahue was a killer.

Max smiled a little to himself. Knowing that answered a lot of the questions he'd been mulling over. It seemed to explain why Donahue was hanging around. He was working.

Somebody had hired him to end the career of Max Trueblood.

Ernie's voice broke into his thoughts. "You want a Polaroid, it'll be twenty-five more."

"No need. I know what he looks like."

Ernie stood and shrugged, which probably set the local Richter readings off. "That's the basics. If I dig, maybe there's more."

"I doubt it. This guy is pretty basic."

"Okay. There's a hunk of fresh pecan pie back here, if you're up to it."

"Why not," Max said. "That can't do any more harm than what I've done already."

Ernie chuckled, sounding like somebody was shaking nails inside a rusty bucket.

Max had the pie and a cup of strong coffee as he mused things over. The whole thing was really pretty amusing, if you thought about it. Jeremiah Donahue was going to kill him.

Well, he was going to try. The question now was, what should he do about it?

His musing provided no answer for that question.

2

Maybe these people were just all hung up on games. Cloak and dagger stuff. Why else would they keep giving him all these stupid instructions? He had, for chrissake, a perfectly good telephone back in his room, but did that satisfy them? Oh, no. Instead of sitting at home, safe and sound, he was standing by a phone booth in the middle of the fucking night waiting for a call.

And not just any phone booth, either. Had to be this very one, which was sitting smack in the middle of a neighborhood where he'd rather not have been alone at this hour. Or any hour, to tell the honest to God truth. Felt like he was Dr. Fucking Livingstone or something, in the middle of the freaking jungle.

If he hadn't brought the gun, which was tucked into the pocket of his jacket, he would have been even more nervous than he already was. Which was pretty damned nervous.

Jeremiah paced outside the booth, inhaling from the latest in a chain of cigarettes. If he didn't get shot on this damned job, he reflected, lung cancer would probably finish him off.

There was an out-of-order sign hung on the front of the booth, but he had a feeling that was just a nice little touch added by whatever perverted mind was behind this whole thing.

Them and their stupid games.

He wished the phone would ring.

And, finally, it did.

Jeremiah pushed into the booth and picked up the receiver. "Yeah?"

"Donahue?"

"No, it's Princess Fucking Di."

"Still got that great sense of humor, I see." The voice belonged to Ichabod, the same man he'd met with in the park. "So what progress do you have to report?"

"Max—Trueblood, I mean—he just hired out to Marberg."

"Hmmm." Ichabod didn't sound surprised. "What for?"

"To off Nick Costa."

"Trueblood let you know that?"

Jeremiah gave a snort. "Let me know it, hell, I was right there when the fucking deal went down."

Ichabod gave a soft chuckle. "I can't believe that."

"Well, you better believe it, because I was on the scene through the whole thing."

"I hate to admit it, Donahue, but you're good. Damned good."

Jeremiah was beginning to feel claustrophobic in the small booth. "Good at what? I haven't done anything yet."

"Hell, you haven't. You got inside. Close enough to Trueblood. That's the first step."

He leaned out, trying to get some air into his lungs. "Yeah, I did that. It wasn't hard."

"If you say so. Mr. Tadzio will be pleased."

"Terrific. So what next?"

"Next you wait."

"For what?"

Ichabod sighed. "For him to kill Costa, of course. When that happens, you fulfill the contract."

"I kill Max."

"See, you are smart. Keep in touch."

"I'll send a love note," Jeremiah snapped. Then he hung up.

He stepped out of the booth and took a deep breath.

Something with a very sharp point poked his spinal column lightly. "Move, muthafucker, and I'll cut you bad."

"I'm not moving," he whispered.

"Gimme your bread."

Even with all his years in the city Jeremiah had never been mugged before. He'd heard people, even men who would not have been afraid of much, talk about the fear of something like this, the unknown, random attacker. A taste of bitter bile rose up in his throat. "Okay, okay, just take it easy, okay? Just don't do anything stupid."

Another voice, even younger-sounding than the first, said, "Kill him, why not? Kill the fucker."

Jeremiah knew suddenly, blindingly, that he didn't want to die yet. It wasn't really something that he'd thought much about before that very moment. In fact, there had been times, even when he was a kid, that life sucked so completely that dying sounded like the only way to make things better. But now he knew that there was enough good mixed in with the bad. And there was always hope that things would get better.

But not if he was dead.

God, he didn't want to die here, like this, so stupidly on this stinking New York street. If he had to check out, it should be for something, some purpose. Otherwise the dying would be as meaningless as his life.

"I'm getting the money," he muttered. "Hold your fucking horses."

"Kill him, kill him, kill him," the childish voice chanted over and over, like it was a damned mantra.

His fingers closed around the gun that he had somehow forgotten was there. Without taking time to think about what he was doing and maybe risking losing his guts, he yanked the gun out and, in the same moment, spun around.

The two boys standing there just stared at him. Neither was sixteen; the smaller one looked about twelve. The older one was holding the knife, but he dropped it immediately.

"You wanna kill me?" Jeremiah said, his voice low and hard-edged. "You the son of a bitch who wants to kill me? Try it, fucker, just try it."

"Don't shoot, mister," the taller boy said. "Don't shoot. He didn't mean nothing. He was only kiddin', tryin' to scare you. We just was after your bread, that's all. We wasn't gonna hurt you."

Jeremiah was holding on to the gun with both hands so that they couldn't see how he was shaking. "Take off," he said. "Take off. Get the hell out of here, you little bastards. I'll kill both of you if you don't disappear now."

After staring at him for one more instant, openmouthed and vague-eyed, both boys turned and ran. Their tennis shoes made hard slapping sounds in the empty street. In only seconds they were gone.

Jeremiah took a deep breath. Then, very carefully, he put the gun back into his pocket and starting walking toward the subway.

three:

just a coupla tough
white guys hanging out

1

Once or twice a week, instead of cooking breakfast for himself, Max would take his *Times* and go down to the diner on the corner. The food he was served there wasn't as good as what he could do at home, but he enjoyed the break in his routine.

This morning he was still sipping the orange juice, waiting for his eggs and the rest of the meal, when a shadow fell across the words of Tom Wicker's column. Max glanced up and saw a familiar face. "Good morning," he said to Aaron Temple.

"Max. It's been a while." Temple gestured toward the empty chair. "You mind?"

"Not at all. Be my guest."

Temple sat. He took off his glasses and started to clean them with a paper napkin.

"You just dropped in for breakfast, I guess?" Max said.

"Hmm" was the cop's only reply. He replaced his glasses and then spent the next moments attracting the attention of the harried waitress, managing eventually to extricate a cup of coffee. When it came, he sampled it and nodded. Then he looked across the table. "Retirement must agree with you, Max. You're looking good."

"Thank you. Yes, the golden years, as they say, are great."

"Really?"

Max finished the juice. "Frozen," he said. He shook his head. "Why can't they squeeze fresh?"

"It's the instant age," Aaron said.

"Right, of course. Aaron," Max said then, "if the choice is yours to make, don't do it. Retire, I mean. It leaves a great deal to be desired. A man gets a little bored. And a bored man does crazy things."

"Uh-huh. So you're bored. Is that why you're going back to work?"

"Me? Going back to work? Old friend, I think maybe your sources are feeding you bad stuff. Even if I wanted to do something like that, who would hire an old man like me?"

"Somebody who was smart enough to want the best."

Max inclined his head slightly. "Why, thank you."

"For instance, Sam Marberg."

"I never really thought old Sam was all that smart, actually," Max said. He smiled at the waitress as she set a plate of eggs and ham in front of him. "You pick his name out of a hat, did you?"

"Are you into playing games these days? I know damned well that you spotted us outside Marberg's place."

"Oh, that. Yeah, I saw you, but I figured you were just keeping tabs on Sam. Not me."

"Not you? Or the guy with you?"

"Nope." Max knew that Aaron was fishing for a name, but he ignored that. "I'm right, aren't I? It was Marberg you were interested in."

Aaron smiled. "Originally, yes. But when I saw you, I got curious."

"You know, there seems to be a lot of that going around these days. Curiosity." Max took a bite and chewed before speaking again. "We were just having lunch, that's all."

"Socializing, like?"

"Right, Aaron. When you're retired like me, you have a lot

of time for things like that. Lunch. Making new friends. Playing games." He spread strawberry jam on a slice of rye bread.

Aaron watched him. "Maybe you're looking for some excitement. Could that be right?"

Max didn't say anything.

Someone stopped by the table, and they both looked up. Aaron finished his coffee in a gulp. "Max, this is my partner, Cody Blaine."

Max, chewing toast, nodded.

Blaine looked young to be a homicide dick, but then everybody looked young these days. He was wearing white duck pants, a lime-green knit shirt, and an unhappy expression. "Trueblood," he said curtly.

Max smiled. "I get the feeling that your partner's not real crazy about me, Aaron," he said.

Blaine grimaced. "Is there any reason why I should be?"

"Probably not. But good manners are always nice."

"Yes, sir," he said.

Aaron seemed to be enjoying himself.

"You ready or what?" Blaine said then.

"Ready." Aaron stood. "Nice talking to you, Max. Take care."

"Always."

"And if you get the feeling that somebody's watching, it's probably only me."

"That's a comfort."

They walked out. It looked like Blaine was complaining about something. Max watched them go, then debated the caloric dangers of another slice of toast. To hell with it, he decided, reaching for the jam.

"What'd those cops want?" Jeremiah dropped into the just vacated chair.

"Good morning," Max said.

"I was standing outside and saw them. What's wrong?"

"Calm down, Jeremiah. For chrissake, nothing's wrong.

Aaron Temple and I have been rattling each other's chains since before you were born. We enjoy it. He just stopped in to say hello."

Donahue was still looking uneasy. "That's all?"

"Yes. Oh, well, he also wanted to find out what we were doing at Marberg's the other day."

"Damn."

"Take a deep breath, kiddo, and calm down."

"It's not easy to stay calm when the heat's crawling around."

Max put the lid back on the jam pot. "You know, Jeremiah, I wouldn't want to do anything to shatter your fragile ego, but the cops are not crawling around you. They don't even know who the hell you are."

Jeremiah scowled. "Well, I know who I am. I'm the guy standing right next to you."

"You put yourself there, buddy boy," Max said genially. "So don't whine to me about it." He glanced around at the emptying diner. "You eat?"

Jeremiah shook his head. "Not hungry."

"We have a busy day ahead. You eat. Didn't your mother ever tell you that breakfast is the most important meal of the day?"

"The only things my mother ever told me were not to go in swimming right after eating, watch out for dirty needles, and always use a rubber when I screw a whore."

"Well, that's all good advice, but here's some more: Always eat a good breakfast." Max waved the waitress over again and ordered a number four—juice, eggs, bacon, and toast.

They sat in silence until the juice was delivered.

"Cops at breakfast," Jeremiah said finally. "Jesus."

Max studied the strangely pale face and the nervous, darting eyes. "You want to cut through the crap, Jeremiah, and tell me what's really bothering you?"

There was more silence, until Donahue sighed. "I got mugged last night."

"That's a hazard of life in the city."

"I pulled my piece and chased them off."

"Good."

"Yeah."

Max frowned. "I say good, and you agree, but your face doesn't look very cheerful."

Jeremiah stared at the just delivered plate of eggs as if they were foreign objects. "It just gave me a very funny feeling. Not like what I expected. The whole thing didn't make me feel . . . oh, tough. Which is a dumb word. But you know what I mean, don't you, Max?"

Holy Mother of God, Max thought, *how the hell did I get myself into this?* Whatever the hell "this" was. It takes a real idiot to complicate his life so much on purpose.

"Yes," he said. "I know what you mean. You didn't feel tough. Eat your eggs."

Jeremiah lifted the fork and took a reluctant bite.

"You ever point a gun at anybody before, Donahue?"

He kept his eyes on the plate. "Sure," he said. "Of course."

Some people might have believed him.

Max thought about advising him to maybe lose the gun and walk around with a plastic bomb in his pocket. But he thought it might be better to keep that little piece of information to himself, at least for the moment.

So all he did was pass the catsup.

Cody sat behind the wheel of the car, practically lighting one cigarette off the remains of another. He was also humming.

Aaron just slouched in the passenger seat, gratefully inhaling the smoke that drifted his way. Finally, exasperated, he said, "Jesus, you're twitchy."

"Who the hell wouldn't be?"

"I know you think we're wasting time."

"Yeah."

"So what the hell would you rather be doing, Joe Friday?"

"I don't know," he admitted. "But sitting here while those creeps have brunch is not my idea of a morning well spent."

"Patience, my boy, patience."

Cody grunted.

Before the level of conversation could deteriorate any further, they were saved by the radio. The metallic voice blandly informed them that there was a dead body awaiting their arrival behind a liquor store twenty blocks away.

The news seemed to cheer Cody visibly. "Breaks the monotony, anyway," he said, tossing the cigarette out the window and reaching for the ignition. "And who knows," he added, "maybe your old pal Max offed this one."

Aaron settled in for one of Cody's usual Indy-style rides to the crime scene. "If Max did," he said, "we'll never be able to prove it."

2

Jeremiah had followed him willingly enough from the diner and walked along without, for once, asking questions. But when he saw their destination, he stopped. "What are we doing here?"

Max opened the door and waved him through. "This is Al's Gym," he said.

"I read that on the sign. But it's not what I asked."

"We're here because I need to work out. It's been a while, and I always like to get in shape before a job."

"You don't look like you've ever been out of shape, if you ask me."

Max gave him a glance. "Well, I haven't let myself fall apart like some people, but I need to hone the edges a little. What about you?"

"Me?"

"What kind of shape are you in?"

"Not bad." He grinned. "For the kind of shape I'm in."

"Oh, great. That sure gives me a lot of confidence."

"Hey, I'm just going along for the ride, anyway, right?"

"Whatever you say, Donahue. But maybe you ought to remember that, as a rule, passengers don't make a whole lot of money."

The old gym smelled the way old gyms always did, the same way it had smelled for all the years that Max had been coming here. A lot of top contenders used to train under Al's skilled eyes, but that was a while ago. Now the gym had fallen on hard times, but Max still came. Once, a few years earlier, he'd tried one of the fancy new health clubs. It only took a single visit for him to realize that he belonged right back here.

The elderly black man grinned when he saw who had come in, and limped toward them. "Mr. Trueblood, how you been keeping? How's the right holding up?"

"Holding up pretty good, Al, considering. I just came in to work up a sweat today."

"That's fine, that's fine. We don't want all that healthy muscle turning flabby. Kills a lot of men your age, you know, getting soft and flabby does."

"I know," Max said, regretting that last slice of toast with jam. "This here is a friend of mine. Think you could round up some sweats for him?"

Al allowed as he probably could, and in a few minutes he had. Jeremiah took them from him with mumbled thanks and followed Max into the locker room. As they both changed, Max was aware that Donahue's expression was becoming increasingly skeptical.

The gym was empty this morning, except for Al himself, who was busy sweeping the floor. Max found himself looking forward to this.

He was smiling as he bent to lace his Keds.

Jeremiah was wishing fervently that he hadn't been practically forced to eat those eggs earlier. Frankly, his nerves were a little on edge, what with all that had happened over the last several days. That tension, combined now with the stink of

old sweat and rancid socks that hung in the air, was tugging at
his gut. God, that was all he needed, a flare-up of the damned
ulcer that had kept him chugalugging Maalox since he was
sixteen.

Still, he tried to look enthusiastic as he rubbed his hands
together and said, "Okay, what now, Jack LaLanne?"

"Nothing fancy. We'll just work the floor for a while."

"Wonderful."

"How long has it been since you jumped rope?"

"Gosh, Miz Scarlett, I don't know nothing 'bout jumpin' no
rope."

"You're a regular Milton Berle, aren't you?" Max picked up
a rope and tossed it to him. "Jump." He picked up a second
rope and started jumping himself.

In a couple of minutes, while Max seemed unaffected,
Jeremiah was gasping hoarsely for breath. He stopped
jumping and leaned against the wall. "Okay," he said with
difficulty. "I'm in shape. If I get into any better shape, I'm
liable to croak. All we have to do is shoot the son of a bitch,
not beat him in a footrace."

"Jeremiah, if you want to get along in this business, you
better learn right now that details are important. They're
crucial, in fact."

"Details. Right, Max. I've got that." Christ almighty, maybe
this was a very clever way of taking him out before he could
hit Max. The perfect murder. Coroner would say, this fool
died from too much exercise. He wouldn't put such a scheme
past the old bastard. Jeremiah briefly considered the satisfaction of planting a small package in Max's locker. Blow the
sadistic creep into smithereens. That would teach him.

Max just smiled at him. "You ready?"

"For what?"

There was no answer. Max only walked away.

He followed Max to one corner of the room where the wall
was lined with mirrors. Al kept the glass shining. "You want to

get us a couple pairs of sixteen-ouncers, please?" Max asked the watching old man.

Jeremiah watched with growing disbelief as Max put one pair of the boxing gloves on his hands and then as Al helped Max don the others. "Ever shadowbox?" Max asked him.

Jeremiah shook his head.

"Okay. The important thing is to keep your feet steady, with the weight evenly balanced." Max demonstrated. "Like that. Got it?"

"Yeah, sure." When Al was safely back across the room, tending to his sweeping once again, Jeremiah leaned toward Max. "We're not gonna shadowbox Costa to death, are we, sir?" he stage-whispered.

The smile Max gave him had a sharp edge. "We are going to do whatever I fucking well say we are, right?"

"Oh, right. Absolutely."

They spent ten minutes or so bobbing and weaving in front of the mirrors, each man throwing a volley of rapid punches. Jeremiah was breathing heavily by the time they quit.

There was a brief, merciful pause before Max waved him over to a heavy bag. "Let me see your right," he said.

Jeremiah slugged the bag.

Max nodded. "Okay. Pretty good. Now do it the right way. Keep your wrist straight, pull back, put your shoulder into it. And by the way, can I ask you something?"

"What?"

"Just what the hell have you been doing with your life, anyway?"

Jeremiah wiped at the sweat on his face. "Stealing cars, dammit. I don't beat people up, I just hot-wire like a son of a bitch. Lemme tell you something, Max. See, I grew up in a very rough neighborhood. The girls on the street could clean your clock without even messing up their eye makeup. So I learned pretty fast that my best weapon was my mouth. Talking saved my ass a lot."

"I believe it. Hit the bag again."

He did, and after a couple of times he began to enjoy the sensation. Every punch seemed to shake his entire body. Finally Max stopped him. Jeremiah turned. "How's that?"

"Much better. You could maybe lick the girls now."

"Thanks a lot."

Max waited until he was taking in oxygen normally again, then led him over to the boxing ring. He climbed in, then turned to look down at Jeremiah.

Jeremiah eyed him. "You're kidding, aren't you?"

"Get in here."

Jeremiah sighed and did as ordered. They faced each other in the center of the ring. Jeremiah held his gloved hands awkwardly in front of him. "Now what?"

"Hit me, you jackass."

"What?"

"Hit me."

The first moves in the match were tentative. He had never felt so uncoordinated. His hands, which he could usually trust to do pretty much what he wanted, including fooling around with some pretty dangerous devices, felt as if they were holding on to a couple of bowling balls; and his feet, unused to the surface of the ring, tingled strangely, then seemed to die. He was soon gasping for breath again.

When Max landed a sharp jab to his gut, Jeremiah stood still, giving him a dirty look. Max hit him again.

So the old fart wanted to play rough? Fine.

Jeremiah came out swinging, forgetting finesse and everything else Max had just taught him. He was, for the moment, back in the alleys of Hoboken. His silver tongue had failed him, forcing a fight. He came at Max like an enraged windmill.

One lucky blow was all it really ever took, and this one landed squarely on Max's nose. Immediately, there was a gushing of blood. Max swore and backed away, reaching for the towel hanging on the ropes.

Jeremiah lowered his hands. "Shit. Hey, Max, you okay? I didn't mean to do that."

"Of course, I'm okay, stupid. Forget it. I told you to hit me. That's the point of boxing."

Jeremiah used his forearm to wipe at the sweat trailing down his face. "But that was a dirty punch. I wasn't following the rules."

"That was a dumb lucky punch. And the only rule out there is surviving, buddy boy," Max said, his voice muffled by the towel. "You better not forget that."

Jeremiah kept apologizing all the way back to the locker room where Max finally got the bleeding stopped. They showered in silence, dressed quickly, and left the gym.

As they reached the sidewalk Jeremiah said that he was really sorry.

Max stopped, glaring at him. "Donahue, shut the fuck up about it, willya?"

He shut up.

The shortcut, which had been Jeremiah's suggestion, turned out not to be such a great idea, after all. "Who knew the dagos were having a carnival?" he said by way of apparent apology.

Max hadn't wanted to take the damned shortcut in the first place, but he also didn't want to be the kind of person who would say "I told you so," so he didn't say anything at all. He just sighed and reached for a cigarette.

It was apparently some holy day or other, and the entire block had been closed off to traffic so the street could be filled with concessions and religious displays.

Jeremiah lifted his head and sniffed the air. "Smells good, though."

Max dropped the match into the gutter. "I wouldn't know, because my nose isn't exactly operating at full power."

Jeremiah looked sheepish. "Hey, lemme get us some lunch, okay?"

"I thought you were broke."

"Well, mostly. But I can probably spring for some food. Come on."

Reluctantly, Max followed him into the crush of the crowd. After a brief deliberation they stopped in front of a booth selling pizza by the slice. Jeremiah quickly totaled the prices and decided he could manage two slices apiece, plus some beer. Balancing the paper plates and cups carefully, they managed to find an empty stoop and decided to claim it as a dining post.

"When I was a kid," Jeremiah reminisced through a huge mouthful of pepperoni and cheese, "these church things were a real gold mine. I usta come over from Jersey special on holy days and make a pile, just lifting wallets."

"Those were the good old days," Max said absently, his eyes scanning the crowd. You never knew who was going to show up at one of these things. The damnedest people had religion."

"Right."

He turned his gaze back to Donahue. "Have you ever stopped to think, Jeremiah, that just maybe you've already reached your particular niche in life?"

Jeremiah frowned. "What are you saying? That I'm too stupid to do anything except boost cars or lift a few wallets?"

"Did I say that?" Max finished his pizza and wiped his mouth with a crumpled paper napkin. "I didn't say anything like that. But not everybody is cut out for every kind of job. That's all I meant."

"I'm going to do fine," Jeremiah said. "Don't you worry about me."

Max met his gaze for a moment. "If you can handle it, terrific," he said.

"I can handle it." Jeremiah blinked and looked away.

Max nodded. He surveyed the scene again, and his eye was caught by one of the brightly painted carny booths down the block. "Come on," he said suddenly, getting up and moving toward it.

Jeremiah quickly gathered the trash from their lunch and threw it into a can, then followed him.

Max stopped in front of the target-shooting booth.

Jeremiah looked at it, then at him. "More games, Max?"

"Just don't point the damned gun at me," Max said. He handed a couple of bills to the old man running the game, and the man gave him the target rifle. "A little refresher course couldn't hurt either one of us, could it?" he said.

"Right."

The parade of ducks moved across the back of the booth in cheerful silence. There were three shots in the gun, and as Max quickly fired, three ducks flipped out of sight. The old guy behind the counter looked a little dismayed but handed him a stuffed dog, anyway.

Max looked at it, then watched as Jeremiah picked up the rifle. "Pulls a little to the left," he said. "Don't be nervous, kiddo." He got a dirty look.

Jeremiah fired three times quickly.

"Too bad," the old man said. "You got another buck, try again, maybe you hit one."

Max put a dollar on the counter. "Do it again, Jeremiah," he said. The tone in his voice left no choice about it.

Again he missed all three shots and another bill appeared.

"Max," Jeremiah said.

"Do it."

This time he managed to hit one duck. There was a line of sweat visible above his upper lip.

Another dollar.

He knocked over two ducks.

Max nodded. "Okay." He put one more bill down but this time picked up the gun himself. Almost without seeming to aim at all, he knocked over all three ducks. The old man grimaced but held out another dog. This time Max shook his head.

They walked away from the booth.

Jeremiah watched his own feet move for a while, then looked up. "You made your point, Max."

"What point was that?"

"That just because I got lucky in the gym before, I shouldn't start thinking I'm any match for the great Max Trueblood. That was the point of all this, wasn't it?"

"I don't know. Maybe. But maybe I just wanted to be sure you could handle a gun." After a moment Max smiled faintly. "But probably I was making a point."

"Oh, you're still king of the mountain, Max, don't worry about that."

Max stopped walking and glanced at his watch. "Getting late, Jeremiah, and I've got things to do. I'll see you tomorrow, okay?"

Jeremiah looked a little puzzled at the sudden brush-off, but all he said was, "Okay, Max."

Max tossed the damned stuffed dog through the air toward him, and Jeremiah just managed to catch it. "You take the dog."

"What the hell should I do with it?"

Max grinned at him. "Teach it to kill, why don't you, kiddo?"

Then he turned and walked away.

3

When Jeremiah spoke to Ichabod Crane later that day, he told the man that he wanted to see Tadzio again. There was a lot of static, but in the end he got his way.

The meet was set up for that night, at a social club in Little Italy. The place was shabby and there wasn't much going on. Some old men were playing dominoes in one corner. The doorman pointed him across the room to where Tadzio was sitting in a booth drinking wine. With him were two men that Jeremiah didn't know. They both got up and left when he sat.

"Didn't mean to break up the party," he said.

Tadzio didn't respond; he also didn't offer to share any of the wine with him. Maybe he was listening too hard to Perry Como on the jukebox. Finally, though, Tadzio spoke. "You got some kind of problem, Jerry? Some kinda complication with the job?"

Jeremiah picked up a breadstick from the basket on the table. "Not a complication, exactly. It's just . . ."

"I don't have all night, Jerry. You got a problem, spit it out."

He was making crumbs from the breadstick. "Okay." He took a deep breath. "You know, sir, this Trueblood, he's not doing anything to you. He never even mentions you. The job, killing Costa, that doesn't have anything to do with us. So maybe what I'm trying to say is that possibly killing him like you said isn't really necessary." He finished in a rush, then took in more air.

Tadzio finished the glass of wine, then very carefully dabbed at his mouth with a linen napkin. "Mr. Donahue, I'm gonna have to be very blunt with you."

"Okay."

"This is not making me happy. You came to me, remember, wanting a job. Something important, you said. And you promised to do whatever I asked. You remember that conversation?"

"I remember."

"Good." He paused to pour more wine from the carafe. "But now you come here telling me the job I gave you is not necessary. Are you trying to tell me my business?"

Jeremiah wished that he could be somewhere else, any-place else, as long as it was away from the harsh voice and frigid gaze. "No, it's not that. I'm not trying to tell you your business. I just thought—" He stopped, swallowed, then started again. "Look, maybe what it comes down to is, maybe I'm not right for this particular job. That's all."

Tadzio smiled icily. "But that's not all. You understand that the plans have all been made. Things have been set into motion. There are many people involved."

"But somebody else could probably—"

Tadzio raised a hand and Jeremiah shut up. "There is no going back. Understand?"

Jeremiah stared at him for a moment, then nodded slowly. "Yes," he said in a soft voice. "I understand."

"Good. We shall expect to be kept informed of how matters are progressing."

"Okay," Jeremiah said. Okay. What else could he say? Tadzio nodded.

The meeting was over.

Jeremiah poured himself a glass of the cheap whiskey he kept under the sink but didn't add any water like he usually did. He sat on the bed to drink it.

Things were not going the way he had thought they would. Which was putting it mildly.

The stuffed dog was staring at him with black button eyes. He toasted it.

What it all came down to was this: Jeremiah had never met either Alphonse or Ngo. He knew absolutely nothing about either one of them, beyond the fact that one drove a Buick and one a BMW, although he couldn't remember now which was which. He hadn't needed to know any more than that.

And if he had bothered to think about it at all, which he didn't really allow himself to do, he would have looked upon what he was doing as more of an exercise in mechanics than murder. He created the bombs, sure, and he planted them. But when the devices exploded, Jeremiah Donahue was somewhere else altogether. It never touched him. And so he had convinced himself that killing a man was a simple thing to do.

But Alphonse and Ngo had been faceless creeps to him, nothing more. He never knew them at all.

This was much different. This was so hard.

The knock at the door startled him. "Yeah?"

"It's only me, Jerry." Sandy's voice said from the hallway.

"What you want?"

"Just thought maybe you'd like some company."

"No. Not tonight, sweetheart."

She went away.

Jeremiah began to shake. Or maybe he'd been shaking for a long time and he just hadn't noticed it. He gulped down the rest of the whiskey, burning a trail through his gullet, but that didn't help. Despite the fact that it was a muggy, hot night, he crawled under the blanket and curled there, trying to stop shaking.

four:
is real life
anything like this?

1

Jeremiah was still in bed the next morning when the pounding started on his door. He wasn't asleep—in fact, he hadn't slept much all night—but he was reluctant to actually leave the bed and face all that would mean. He didn't need to read his horoscope to know that this day promised to turn into a real bastard before it was over.

When the loud knocking started, he rolled over and glared at the door. "Who is it?"

"The tooth fairy."

Jeremiah got up and pulled his jeans on before going to the door and flinging it open. "Nobody should try to be funny so fucking early in the morning," he said. His mouth tasted terrible and he belched, recalling the bad whiskey.

"It's not all that early," Max said.

"And you're not all that funny, but come in anyway. Siddown." Without any further pleasantries he went into the bathroom.

He stared at himself in the mirror. "You're getting old, Jeremiah," he said. The haggard face looking back didn't disagree. "Damn."

* * *

Alone, Max took the opportunity to study the room. God, it was depressing. And familiar. He could well remember living in places like this one. For a long time.

He walked around, opening some drawers and checking the closet. There was a locked strongbox on the shelf and he picked it up to look at, then set it back in place carefully. If this guy liked to play around with bombs, there was no telling what might be in the damned thing.

As he took in the crummy furniture and peeling paint, Max felt a not altogether comfortable sense of kinship with the man who occupied this space. Maybe they were more alike than he really wanted to recognize.

He found the gun in a drawer and looked at it carefully. Cheap and not very reliable.

Maybe, when he'd been Jeremiah's age, he might have been dumb about some things too. Maybe. But he certainly didn't go around getting chummy with guys he was planning to hit. Max didn't think that was very wise.

He made the bed, then sat down to thumb through the *TV Guide*.

By the time he had taken the usual lukewarm shower which was all the plumbing provided, brushed his teeth, and shaved quickly, Jeremiah was feeling more awake but not much better otherwise. When he came out of the bathroom, Max was sitting on the bed, except that it was a couch again. "A real garbage heap, right?" Jeremiah said, embarrassed.

"I've seen worse."

"Not many, probably." He perched on the back of the couch. "So what's up? How come you're here?" It occurred to him to wonder how Max had found out where he lived, but then he decided it was probably better not to ask.

"I'm here because we have work to do."

"Work?"

"Christ, you say the word like you're allergic or something. Yes, work. The hit on Costa comes down tomorrow."

"So soon?" Jeremiah heard his voice crack.

"We'll be ready. Besides, if we wait much longer, the sneaky bastard will die of old age and cheat us out of our money."

"Yeah, I guess." He rubbed the worn, nubby surface of the upholstery with his hand. "Yeah, okay. Tomorrow. But can we take time for breakfast first, please?"

Max nodded. "Sure. I didn't eat yet."

Jeremiah got busy with the hot plate and boiled some water for coffee. While that was cooking, he took a box of two-day-old jelly doughnuts from the cupboard and set them on the table in front of the couch. Finally, he rinsed a couple of mugs clean, spooned instant coffee into each one, and set them down as well. "Out of milk," he said.

Max studied the meal, his face unreadable. "Eating like this will rot your brain, you know, kiddo."

"Sorry, but it's the cook's fucking day off, or I'd'a served you eggs Benedict. That's what I usually have."

Max shook his head. "Don't get your feelings hurt, stupid. I only meant that you have to learn to live right or it won't be worth the trip."

Jeremiah spoke through a bite of stale doughnut. "What trip is that, Max?"

"The one to the grave, of course." Max smiled.

After a moment Jeremiah laughed, scattering powdered sugar.

They took the subway and then walked without hurrying to a park way the hell in the middle of Brooklyn. Max apparently knew just where they were going, but he didn't seem inclined to share that information. Jeremiah thought about asking some questions, but because he didn't want either to raise suspicions or look stupid, he just kept quiet.

The park was part of some private club, and the whole place

was surrounded by a high brick wall. Max told him that the wall had been built by a bunch of monks who used to have a monastery inside the barrier. The place was guarded now by guys who didn't look like they had any religion at all, unless maybe it involved sacrificing those foolish enough to try to penetrate the security of the joint.

After they had walked around the entire wall once, Max paused long enough to buy a *Times* from a bored vendor. Then he led the way to a bench set across the street from the gate. They sat and Max opened the paper.

Jeremiah sat still for about two minutes, then he sighed and leaned forward, resting his arms on his knees. Boring. He knew that some old men liked to sit on benches and read the newspaper, but Max didn't seem like the type. Next thing he knew, they'd be feeding the fucking pigeons.

He sighed again. "Max, what're we doing here?"

"If you're planning to kill a man," Max said without looking up from his reading, "it's probably a good idea to know something about him. About his habits."

"Yeah, so?"

"So, Mr. Costa should be turning up very soon. According to my information, he plays boccie here every day when the weather is good. So, while I trust my source, I never trust anybody completely. I like to check everything out for myself. Details, Jeremiah, details."

"Details. I guess that's why you're the best, right, Max?"

"That's part of it."

"What's the rest?"

Max eyed him over the top of the paper. "I should give away all my trade secrets?"

Jeremiah smirked. "Hey, you're retired, aren't you? So why should it matter?"

"It doesn't really, not to me. But I had to find out everything for myself, the hard way. That builds character. Why the hell should I make it easy for you?"

"Some friend you are," Jeremiah muttered.

Max just shrugged.

Jeremiah straightened and sat back against the bench.

Some friend. Oh, yeah. And just what the hell was that supposed to mean? You don't have friends in this business; isn't that what the old master himself had said?

And how much do you trust me, Mr. Trueblood?

He closed his eyes and let the sun warm his face. Damn. Whoever the hell invented life in the first place should have done a little more tinkering. As he saw it, the whole thing had some great big flaws.

"Snap to, kiddo," Max said in a low voice. "Here comes the Ancient Order of Sicilian Boccie Players and Scumbags."

Jeremiah opened his eyes and looked.

Three black limos approached the gate, which opened as if by magic, and then the cars disappeared inside. Max frowned. "Problem number one is getting into that place," he said.

"Yeah," Jeremiah agreed. "I'd say so."

"Any ideas?"

"Me? No. I broke into the movies a few times and into a lot of garages in my life, but that's about it."

"This is how you plan on earning your cut? By not having any ideas?"

Jeremiah shrugged.

"Okay," Max said finally. "We'll have to go in early. Like four A.M."

"The place will still be guarded, won't it?"

"Of course, but everybody lets down a little at four o'clock in the morning. So we get in then and pick our spot. Wait for Costa to show up, by which time we're set. How does that sound?"

"Except for having to be up so early, fine, I guess."

Max got up suddenly and they walked around the block again, then crossed the street to stand by the rear gate. This one probably wasn't used, because it was heavily padlocked. There was a guard, of course, but at the moment he was perched on the front of a shiny Toyota, talking to a blonde in a tennis dress. Max snorted.

From this vantage point they could see the boccie players, although it was too far away for a good shot. "The one in the blue pants," Max said, "that's Nick Costa."

Nicholas Costa was a big deal, Jeremiah knew that, but from here he didn't look like so much. He was just a short, fat man with gray hair and glasses. He and everybody else in the group looked at least seventy years old.

Jeremiah pointed with his index finger, keeping his hand low. "Bang, bang, you're dead," he whispered.

Max looked at him. "You having fun?"

Jeremiah met the gaze. "Not so's anybody could notice," he said.

"Will you recognize Costa the next time you see him?"

"Yes, Max."

"You happen to notice that all the apes in there are armed and probably not too bright?"

"Yes, Max."

Max folded the newspaper brusquely. "Let's go."

They walked away, moving neither too fast nor too slowly, doing nothing that would attract any unwelcome attention, following a shaded sidewalk that led away from the park.

"We'll come this way afterwards," Max said, sounding a little like a teacher attempting to instruct a slightly dim-witted student.

"Okay."

"Are you paying attention to me, Jeremiah?" he asked sharply.

"Sure, Max."

"It won't be so simple tomorrow, you know. Somebody will be chasing us. Maybe even shooting at us. Have you ever been shot at before, kiddo?"

"Yeah. Sort of." If kids with a BB gun counted.

"Right." Max shook his head. "All that food you eat. Jesus, it rots your goddamned brain."

"Gimme a little credit, okay, Max? Christ, I know you're the expert. Why wouldn't I listen to you?"

Max didn't respond to that. Instead, he pointed to a diner across the street. "Come on. My blood sugar gets low, I get touchy."

When they were settled at a table and both had ordered burgers, Max said, "Maybe you're getting scared, is that it?"

Jeremiah opened his mouth to object, then he shrugged instead. "I don't know. Maybe some." His voice turned challenging. "Is there anything wrong with that?"

"Not a damned thing. I'd be worried if you didn't have a nice healthy dose of fear."

"You're probably not scared, though, are you?"

"Me?" Max seemed to think about it. "Not much. But I've been doing this for a long time. I'm careful but not really scared. Anyway, what's the worst that could happen?"

"Somebody could kill you."

"Maybe. But I've been around a long time and nobody has yet."

Jeremiah clenched a fist under the table. "There is one thing you haven't mentioned so far."

"What's that?"

"How the hell do we get out of that place once it's done?"

Max took a swallow of water. "That," he said, "is the real stumbling block in my plan."

"What?" Jeremiah said in fake wonder. "The great Max Trueblood doesn't know what to do?"

He frowned. "I'm working on it."

Jeremiah relaxed a little. "Maybe I could help."

"You think so?"

"A couple of distractions, properly placed, might do the trick."

Max nodded. "Might just. What'd you have in mind, kiddo?"

He took a deep breath. "I could blow something up," he said. "Maybe a car. The wall. Whatever you want."

Max didn't look quite as surprised as he'd hoped. "You could manage that?" was all he said.

"I could manage that," Jeremiah replied flatly. To hell with Trueblood if he couldn't be a little impressed. "I've done it before."

"Yes," Max said with a strange little smile. "I know."

Startled, Jeremiah looked at him, but before he could speak, the burgers arrived. Jeremiah was able to occupy himself with trying to shake catsup out of a stubborn bottle. He pounded the bottom viciously. "I guess the whole thing just seems so . . . so stupid, is all," he managed to say.

"What's that?"

"The killing. The fucking killing."

"You mean, Old Man A hires Old Man B to ice Old Man C? That's what you call stupid?"

"Sure." He finally got a dollop of catsup out. "Don't you?"

"Of course." Max sprinkled salt on his fries, still smiling faintly. "But there is a certain symmetry to it, don't you think?"

"A certain what?"

"Symmetry. Like . . . a nice balanced pattern."

Jeremiah thought about it as he chewed, then he nodded. "Yeah. I see what you mean. But it's still stupid."

Max didn't argue the point.

They ate in silence for several minutes.

"You knew already?" Jeremiah said finally.

"I didn't stay alive so long being stupid, Jeremiah."

When his hamburger was gone, Jeremiah stirred the ice in his Pepsi. "I only want to be somebody," he said suddenly. "I want to do something with my life." He looked up at Max. "What's wrong with that?"

"Not a thing," Max said. "If you've got the balls to carry through on it, not a goddamned thing, kiddo."

Cody realized that he didn't particularly like having a day off, especially in the middle of the week. And most especially when they were right in the middle of something that might turn into a major crime war. He couldn't get over the uneasy feeling that they should have been out there doing something.

Fleetingly, it occurred to him that maybe Mandy was right when she said he was much too wrapped up in the damned job. But almost immediately he dismissed the notion. He liked what he did and it was an important job, so why the hell shouldn't he be involved? Only a bad cop put in his eight hours and went home, dismissing it all from his mind.

Since Mandy was at work, he prowled the small apartment alone, doing some vacuuming and then sitting at the table to make a grocery list.

But when he finally left the apartment in the middle of the afternoon, it wasn't to go over to the store and buy eggs. Instead, he found himself driving all the way out to Aaron's place. But there was no answer, and Aaron's car was gone.

Damn, he thought.

Restless and bored, he made a run past a bowling alley where he knew Aaron spent time, then several bars, but there was no sign of the older man. Where the hell could he have gotten to?

Taking one last shot at it before being forced by default into the frozen foods department, Cody went over to the VFW hall.

Sure enough, Aaron was there, sitting alone at a table with a beer in front of him. He didn't look particularly surprised to see his partner come in. Cody crossed the large room and dropped into the chair opposite him.

"This is a very bad sign, Cody," was all Aaron said.

"What is?"

"Starting to hang around cops even on your day off."

"Maybe I'm just too fucking dedicated."

"Sure," Aaron said. "And do you know where all that goddamned dedication is going to get you?"

"Where?"

"Right to the same place it took me. Nowhere."

Cody heard the bitterness in the words. "Do you regret it, sir?"

"Regret it? Hell, no."

"Well, then?"

"But that's just me. Maybe I'm just too damned stupid for regrets. You might feel altogether differently about it."

"Well, I guess in thirty years or so we'll know about that, won't we?"

Aaron shook his head. "Don't come bitching to me about it thirty years from now, then," he said. "I warned you."

Cody took out a cigarette and took his time lighting it. Then he said, "Aaron, what do you think Max Trueblood is doing back in action?"

"Supplementing social security?"

"Could be," Cody agreed.

They grinned at each other.

After another moment Aaron shrugged. "I think that things are getting very hot. And when things get hot, men do whatever they have to. Somebody needs Max bad. He always sort of aggravated the bosses, but they know how good he is. So somebody made him an offer he couldn't refuse. Although, knowing Max, I can't imagine what that offer would be."

"Why don't I get myself a soda and we can cogitate on it for a while?" It sure as hell beat pushing a cart through the aisles of the A&P.

Aaron seemed agreeable, so Cody got up and went to the bar.

This was a more interesting way to spend the rest of the day than shopping for paper towels and cereal. Mandy would bitch, but he could take her out to dinner and make up for it. Cody picked up his drink and hurried back to the table.

3

Jeremiah gave the cabbie an address down by the docks and settled back in the seat. Max handed him a cigarette. "Thanks."

The driver was listening to a Spanish music station, the volume jacked way up. He seemed completely oblivious to his passengers.

"So where'd you learn this shit?" Max asked.

"What shit?" Jeremiah asked, then he said, "Oh. Books, mostly. There's not much you can't find out in the freaking public library, if you know where to look."

"The library? Jesus. What a thought."

"Yeah, isn't it? Hell, if I wanted to, I could build a goddamned atom bomb. It's all right there, in the books."

"Well, that might be sort of overkill, for our purposes."

"Just a little." Jeremiah inhaled deeply, staring out the window. "The way I figure it, we'll need two devices. Use one on a car. That'll be the first distraction. You'll have to get the shot off almost immediately, because those apes who guard Costa will be all over him pretty fast." He glanced at Max. "Can you do that? Get the shot off almost as soon as the car blows?"

"I think I can probably manage to get the fucking shot off whenever I want to," Max replied somewhat testily. "I've been doing it for a lot of years."

Jeremiah smiled sheepishly. "Yeah, sure. Sorry." He finished the cigarette. "I think the second device should go just after the shot. That's when we get the hell out. What would you think about just blowing the rear gate? We move our asses right out while the dust is still settling."

Max thought about it, then nodded. "I like that. Means we'll have to move quick."

"Right."

They got out of the cab in front of a run-down warehouse. Jeremiah led the way around to the rear of the building, pausing at the door. "Maybe you better wait here, Max," he said. "These guys don't much like new faces."

"Yeah, yeah, whatever."

Max settled on the top step and lit another cigarette. He was a little pissed at being left outside. So the kid was a fucking expert at blowing things up. Big deal. Any idiot with ten fingers and a library card could do the same thing. Where had it gotten him so far? A dump to live in and not much respect, apparently. Max shook his head. Problem was, Jeremiah didn't know how to run his life, that was the problem. He obviously didn't know the best way to market the few skills he seemed to have.

Somebody needed to teach the idiot the facts of life.

Jeremiah spent all afternoon sitting at Max's table working. He didn't talk much, except muttered comments to himself, as he worked with wires and plastic.

Max kept quiet, too, sipping a couple of beers and watching.

It was almost five before Jeremiah slid the chair away from the table and walked into the kitchen for a beer himself. He came back and dropped onto the sofa next to Max.

"All done?" Max asked.

"Yeah."

"Will they work?"

Jeremiah shrugged. "If they don't, you won't have to pay me my cut, how about that?"

"Great. Maybe you'd put that in writing?"

Jeremiah laughed. "I don't think it matters much, does it? If they don't work, I mean."

"Won't matter a fucking bit," Max agreed.

They went to a steakhouse on Fifth for an early dinner. Jeremiah had a raging headache that a drink did little to help. He blamed the pain on his hard work all afternoon, but he knew that wasn't the real reason. Picking at the food in front of him, he wanted to say something, anything, that would maybe ease the tightening band around his skull. But what could he say? There weren't any words that would make this easier.

Tomorrow Max would kill Costa.

Then he would kill Max.

It was that simple.

It was that terrible.

After tomorrow Jeremiah Padraic Donahue would finally be somebody. And, goddammit, that was the way the world worked. Everybody over the age of six knew that. It was like that show he'd watched a couple weeks earlier on the educational station. The program was all about fish, about how the big one ate the little ones, and then an even bigger one would come along and eat him. That was life, and if it worked for the fucking fish, it should also work for people.

Max seemed to be enjoying his steak. He chewed thoughtfully, then said, "Got something for you to do tonight."

Jeremiah tasted the baked potato. "What?" he asked suspiciously.

"Sit on Costa a little. Make sure he does what he's supposed to be doing. Which happens to be going to a birthday party for his wife."

"Why should I do that?"

Max stopped eating and looked at him. "Two reasons. One, because I'm telling you to. And that really should be all you need to know, right?"

Jeremiah nodded.

"But I'll even tell you the second reason, since I'm feeling friendly. If Costa all of a sudden changed his plans, that might mean he's somehow gotten wind of what's going on. That would spook him. And I'd rather know it if we're going after a spooked target. Things get harder under those circumstances. So you just make sure that he's out with the wife having a good time and feeling nice and safe."

"Okay." Jeremiah gave up pretending to eat and pushed the plate away. "And meanwhile, what are you going to be doing?"

"I have to see a man about a gun."

Jeremiah wished he could figure out why the hell Max Trueblood trusted him. Or seemed to trust him, anyway. Maybe he should just ask.

But, no, he couldn't do that because the bastard might actually tell him. And knowing the reasons, whatever they might be, could only make what he had to do even harder.

If that was possible.

When they parted company in front of the restaurant, Max hailed a cab and gave the driver an address on Lenox. That didn't thrill the Arab a lot, but Max just looked at him and they set off.

When they arrived, he paid the man and the cab took off fast. Max knew he'd have a helluva time finding one to go home in.

He went into the apartment building and started climbing. There was a nodding junkie on the third-floor landing, but Max just stepped around him and walked down the hall to the last door. He knocked once, waited ten seconds, then knocked twice again quickly. The rules of the game.

The door was opened by a slender black man. His name was Jocko, and he was one of the best and busiest weapons dealers in the city. But, busy as he was, there was always time to see a valued old customer.

He ushered Max into the flat, which was furnished far more expensively than the exterior of the building would lead one to believe. Jocko lived well. "Blew me away, Max, when I got your message. Never thought you'd be back in the old rat race."

Max shrugged. "Neither did I. And I'm not, really. This is just a onetime thing. My swan song, you might say."

"So we need to make it special, huh?"

"We need to make it right. I don't want to screw up on my last time out." He told Jocko a little about the setup for the job, minus any names, of course, and the man nodded.

"Think I've got just what you need." He left the room.

Max sat on the purple velvet sofa. A little girl who looked about six wandered in. She was wearing pink pajamas with smiling rabbits all over them and high heels that were much too large, and eating a Twinkie. She eyed him, then smiled, showing gaps where teeth should have been. Max nodded at her and she scurried out, much to his relief. Kids made him nervous. You never know what they might see or remember.

It was another few minutes before Jocko returned, carrying a wooden box. "Just got this in," he said. "See what you think of it."

Max lifted the lid of the box and studied the gun inside. Even broken down it looked good. It looked deadly, and he liked a gun to look like just what it was. He took the parts out, one by one, expertly assembled the weapon, and balanced it in his hands. "Feels right. What about a scope?"

"Got a fine Lyman All-American 4-x I can give you a decent price on. Accurate up to about three hundred yards with a good eye behind it. Your eye still good, is it, Max?"

"My eye is fine, thanks. Okay, I'll take this and the scope. Usual ammo allotment. And some kind of case that can travel in public."

He had just the case, a nice piece of work in black leather that he was willing to part with. Max carefully counted out almost two grand before leaving the apartment.

The junkie was still on the landing, but this time Max took a closer look at him, and he saw a pair of sharp black eyes following his departure. Sentry duty. Jocko was no fool.

Max stepped out onto the sidewalk and began the hunt for a cab.

After he had counted the windows in the building across the street and talked to a pair of half-wild cats prowling for their dinner, Jeremiah got pretty bored in the alley behind LaBresca's Italian Restaurant. Max hadn't told him how long to keep this sentry duty going, so even after he'd seen Nick Costa and his heavily guarded party go inside for the noisy festivities, he stayed put.

Just for something to do, he smoked seven cigarettes in a row, making himself a little sick to his stomach. Deliberately, he didn't think about the circumstances of his life at the moment. His old lady used to say something about leaving tomorrow for the devil to worry about, and that definitely seemed the best thing to do with the tomorrow that he was facing.

A man in a white jacket stepped into the alley and tossed something from a bucket into a trash can. Jeremiah stepped back into the shadows. The cook glanced around, as if he'd heard something, then went back inside.

Maybe he'd been here long enough. Costa was inside, presumably having himself a helluva time, so why didn't he just split?

It sounded like a good idea, but before he could act upon it, two guys appeared from somewhere. Jeremiah heard them coming, but while he was deciding whether to turn and confront them or run away, which was his first choice, one of them clipped him and he tumbled like a sacked quarterback. He didn't even get a chance to pull the gun or use any of the fancy moves that Max had taught him.

Some feet poked at him. "Whattcha doing out here, creep?" a voice asked.

"Nothing," he said, trying to stay out of the way of the sturdy shoes.

"We don't like creeps watching us."

"I wasn't watching anybody." He grunted as his ribs were jabbed again. "Hey, look, man, I came back here to take a leak, okay? There a law against that or something? I didn't want to pull it out in the middle of fucking Seventh Avenue."

"That makes sense," the man said. But they kicked him a few more times, anyway, and one of the blows got his nose bleeding. Poetic justice, maybe. "Next time play with yourself somewhere else, got that?"

"I got it," he said.

They went back inside. As the door opened briefly, Jeremiah could hear the band playing "Happy Birthday." Everybody cheered. He got up and limped out of the alley.

Not surprisingly, two cabs passed him by before he managed to flag down a rusted gypsy, the driver of which didn't seem to care if his fare was gushing blood and groaning occasionally.

"Where you going, pal?" the driver asked.

An interesting question. And one for which he had no good answer at the moment. Lacking any other idea, he gave the guy Max's address.

4

Max turned the Charlie Parker over and started the music again. The Bird could always relax him. He poured a Taddy Porter and sat at the table once more to finish cleaning and assembling the gun. He liked to get to know a weapon, even if it was only going to be used once. And when he bought a gun for a specific job, it was only used once.

When he heard the knock at the door, he carefully placed the gun into the case and shut it before going to see who it was. He opened the door and stood there, looking Jeremiah up and down. "Run into a wall, did you, Donahue?" he asked, trying not to feel a twinge of satisfaction as he took note of the bloody nose.

Jeremiah leaned against the wall. "I fucked up, Max. A couple of Costa's boys spotted me, and they weren't happy." He wiped away some blood and looked at him. "Did I screw everything up, Max?"

"Get in here." When he was inside, Max shut and locked the door. "No, I don't think you blew it for us. My bet is, they didn't suspect anything but just pummeled on you for the fun of it."

"Some fun."

"Depends on your taste." Max took a closer look. "Didn't I tell you to keep your goddamned right up?"

"I didn't get the chance."

"Too bad." He went into the bathroom, stuck a towel under the cold water faucet, then squeezed out the excess water and walked back into the living room. "Sit down and wipe your face," he said, handing the damp towel to Jeremiah.

Donahue slumped onto the couch and tried to clean away the blood. There wasn't much that could be done for the shirt.

Max went into the kitchen for some aspirin and orange juice. "Swallow these. You're going to be sore as hell in the morning."

Jeremiah snorted. "Fuck the morning. I'm sore as hell now."

Max used one hand to tip his head back and study the damage to his face. "You'll be okay. Does it hurt to breathe?"

"No, but laughing is a real effort."

Max smiled faintly. "You'll do."

"So we're still a go for tomorrow?"

"Bright and early, sonny boy, bright and early. Which means you better get some sleep. The couch isn't bad." He went to get an extra blanket and pillow, tossing them down next to Jeremiah.

"Thanks."

"Sweet dreams," Max replied. "Charlie can be your lulla-by."

"Charlie?"

"Parker. That's music, in case you didn't recognize it."

Jeremiah shrugged.

Max went into his bedroom. He undressed and sat on the bed for a last cigarette. Well, it was just about time. Pretty soon the world would know if Max Trueblood still had it or if he should go stake out a park bench someplace. Adopt a couple of pigeons.

Everything should go smoothly.

Of course, a lot depended on the wild card in the next room. Max wondered when the hell Donahue was going to make his move.

He crushed out the cigarette and stretched out on the bed. He was asleep almost immediately.

Jeremiah rolled over and read the clock by the moonlight. God, he'd been lying here almost two hours and he hadn't slept at all. His gut was churning, and every time he closed his eyes, the pictures he saw made it worse. Sweet dreams, yeah.

Finally he got up and padded, barefoot, into the kitchen. He found a glass and poured it full of milk, then opened a box of cookies. He sat at the table. Well, things were just great, weren't they? Maybe he should get dressed and just split right now. Leave town. Except that how far could he get with about five dollars? Not nearly far enough.

He heard a noise and looked up to see Max standing there, tying a bathrobe. "What's wrong?"

Jeremiah took a gulp of milk. "My ribs hurt," he mumbled.

"Yeah," Max said. "You look like a guy who's hurting." He sat down across from him and picked up one of the cookies. "Kiddo, let me tell you something. Nothing is easy. Nothing. This kind of life we have sure isn't. The point is, we have to do whatever it takes to get along. Maybe we don't like doing some of it, but that doesn't matter. There's just no goddamned choice."

Jeremiah crumbled a cookie. "Max, I feel like . . . I don't want . . ." He shut up. Dammit, he couldn't say it. He couldn't say anything.

Max just finished the cookie. Surprisingly, he reached across the table and patted Jeremiah's hand. "Don't worry about it," he said. Then he went back to bed.

Jeremiah stayed where he was. Christ, it almost seemed as if Max knew exactly what was going on. But that just couldn't be. No way. Because if he knew what Jeremiah was going to do, wouldn't he just have offed him a long time ago? After all, that's what Max did, for chrissake, he killed people. One jerk more or less couldn't matter to him.

But instead of doing that, instead of doing what he should have, Max was being friendly. Hell, nobody had ever treated him like this, like he was a buddy or something. It just didn't make any sense.

Nothing made any sense these days.

Jeremiah left the milk and cookies where they were and went back to the couch.

EVEN BAD GUYS GET THE BLUES

one:

not exactly
according to plan

1

It was still dark when Max got up. He checked on his guest, who seemed dead to the world, then went in to shower and dress. He put on his usual working clothes—slacks and a sport shirt—which was pretty much the same thing he wore every day. Except that he was careful to avoid bright colors or anything else that might stick in the mind.

He stopped on the way to the kitchen and nudged the sleeping man. "Time's up."

Jeremiah sat up stiffly. His eyes were bleary and puffy, and his face was a pale green shade.

"How're the ribs?"

"I'm okay," he said in a thick voice.

"Hit the can while I make breakfast."

Jeremiah made a face at the mention of food, but he got up obediently and disappeared into the bathroom.

It seemed to Max that the shower ran for a very long time, but at least Donahue looked a little better when he finally emerged. He had donned the same jeans from the day before but not the bloody shirt. Max tossed him an old gray sweatshirt.

"Thanks," he said, pulling it on. At Max's nod he sat. The faint whiskers were gone, and in their place were several fresh nicks. "I can't believe you shave with a straight razor," he complained, touching his chin ruefully. "It's like using a frigging butcher knife."

"I'm used to it," Max said.

Jeremiah surveyed the table, which held coffee, a bowl of fluffy scrambled eggs, and warm cinnamon rolls. "Looks good," he said, obviously making an effort.

Max poured two cups of the strong coffee. "Well, you look like hell."

Jeremiah shrugged. "I'll be okay."

"If you're not okay, Jeremiah, tell me now. I can't afford to have you folding up on me out there. Unless you're really on top of it, stay here and wait for me to come back."

There was something strange in the glance Jeremiah gave him, as if the young man were trying to read his mind. Gauge what he knew. But when he spoke, all he said was "You know, Max, I appreciate the fact that you never call me Jerry. Most people do and I really hate it."

Max looked at him, then shook his head. Jesus H. Christ.

Jeremiah reached for the scrambled eggs. "You need me," he said. "Without me to do my part of this thing, your ass would be burned."

"I don't need you or anybody else," Max replied. "Never did. I'll get the job done with or without your tricks."

His mouth full of eggs, Jeremiah only shrugged.

"Though it'll be easier if your stuff works," Max admitted reluctantly.

Jeremiah smirked.

"Can you do it?"

"Can I do what?"

"Climb the fence, of course. Can you climb the fence?"

They both spoke in whispers, although the guards were in their hut, probably having some wake-up coffee. Max didn't bother to answer the question. It was just about dawn, and the street that ran along the back of the private park was nearly empty.

"Cup your hands," Max said.

"What?"

He leaned closer and spoke in a clipped tone. "Cup your fucking hands, crouch, and then boost me to the top. Pass me the gun case and your bag, then I'll pull you up. Got it?"

Instead of saying anything and aggravating him further, Jeremiah just did as he'd been ordered. Max pulled him up, as promised, and then Jeremiah dropped to the other side. Max handed him both bags. He slipped down then, landing heavily on both knees.

"You okay?" Jeremiah whispered.

"No, I broke my neck," Max answered. "You want to stand here and talk about it?" They moved through the diminishing shadows and stopped behind a thick stand of bushes that sat on a small rise overlooking the area where the boccie game was played. It was a good hiding spot, though a little farther from the rear gate than Max would have liked. But they couldn't afford to be choosy, and at least here they were shielded on three sides by the bushes and to their rear by a large trash can.

There was no time to sit and think about it, anyway.

Jeremiah took one of the bundles out of his bag and, without saying anything to Max, sprinted toward the gate. This was a little different than wiring a car and he started to sweat some before the job was done. He took one step backward and admired the work. The branches from a large old oak tree mostly concealed the explosives from any but the most careful study. He nodded, satisfied, then turned and ran back to the safety of the bushes. He was panting a little as he dropped to the ground next to Max again.

"Go okay?" Max said.

"Sure. Of course. I know what I'm doing."

They waited, mostly in silence, for about thirty minutes,

and then it was apparently time for the changing of the guard. A gray Chevy drove by, parking next to the guards' hut, and two men got out. The night shift emerged and, after a brief conversation, climbed into a brown Ford and left.

After the new arrivals had made a cursory tour of the perimeter, they headed for the hut.

"This place should do something about its security," Jeremiah muttered.

Max half smiled. "I have a feeling they will," he said. "Real soon."

"Yeah." Jeremiah reached for the second package. "Wish me luck," he said.

"Just watch your ass."

He slid out and kept close to the ground all the way to the car, then slipped right under the front of the vehicle. This was easier than wiring the gates had been, technically speaking, but more difficult because he was in greater risk of being heard or seen.

But it all went smoothly. He gave the car an almost affectionate pat. This was going to make a helluva blast.

Now there was nothing to do but wait.

The next several hours passed with painful slowness. Jeremiah was going a little crazy. Max seemed cool, totally on top of the situation, but after so many years of this, Jeremiah figured that he should have been. When the time of the game drew near, he pulled on a pair of thin rubber gloves and opened the leather case. Jeremiah watched him assemble and load the gun.

A foursome showed up and took to the tennis court. The guards were out of their hut now, but the one who was supposed to be watching the rear gate seemed more interested in the game. Somebody's ass was going to be in a sling after this, Jeremiah was willing to bet.

"Max, I have a question."

"Of course you do. What?"

"Do you ever feel bad about it?"

He was checking the scope. "About what?" he said absently.

"Killing people."

Now Max looked at him. "It's what I do. Why should I feel bad?" He set the gun down, flexing his fingers. "Maybe it was hard at first, but I don't even remember. Anyway, I couldn't spend my whole life feeling bad about what I do. That would be stupid."

"Yeah, I guess." Jeremiah peered through the bushes, but no one had appeared for the boccie game yet. "Did you ever kill anybody you knew?"

"Of course. It's a small world."

"Ever kill a friend?"

"What the hell is this, Twenty Questions?"

Jeremiah just looked at him.

Max shook his head. "No, I never killed a friend. But there's a good reason for that. I never had any friends. Better that way."

"Yeah, I can see that." Jeremiah gnawed on his fingernail, wondering why he kept having the feeling that Max was laughing at something. As far as he could see, there wasn't a goddamned thing here that was funny. He leaned forward again. "Here they come."

The arrival of the boccie players seemed to put an end to the conversation. Probably that was just as well, because it was getting dangerous, like trying to work with unstable dynamite. Which was a good way to get hurt bad.

Jeremiah could see the change that came over Max as the moment of action neared. The other man's face was expressionless, except for the eyes. They seemed to turn abruptly harder and darker.

Max picked up the gun. "You be ready to move," he said in a low voice. "Remember how it goes?"

"Yeah, sure."

"Tell me." It was snapped out, an order.

"Out of the park, up the block to the market, through the market, then all the way to the subway."

"And?"

"And once we're out of the park, I don't run. I remember it all, Max."

"Don't forget. And don't fuck up, because if you do, boy, I won't wait. You got that?"

"I've got it."

"Okay."

Jeremiah was a little pissed at being treated like the village idiot. "You just be sure to get the fucking shot off on time," he said.

"I will."

And then he saw why Max Trueblood was the best, why he got the big money. How he had survived so many years in a business with a very high mortality rate. It was pretty simple, actually: The man was a stone-cold killer. He made the shooting of Nicholas Costa seem like nothing more than a job, like any other. And to him that was all it was.

"Blow the car," Max whispered, not looking away from his target.

Jeremiah picked up the radio detonator. "Okay?" he said.

"Do it."

The roar of the blast made the ground shake under them. Someone screamed.

Even though his ears were still ringing from the explosion, the shot was louder than Jeremiah had expected it to be. He was watching through the bushes when it happened. He had just the instant that it took to see one of the boccie players stumble and fall.

"The gate," Max said.

Again he pushed a button, and again the ground shook as a roar filled the air.

Max dropped the gun and took off, Jeremiah right on his heels, almost literally. The cloud of dust and rocky debris from the fence was still floating through the air as they ran through the newly made hole. As they moved, Max peeled the gloves from his hands, pausing just long enough to drop them down the sewer. Behind them, it sounded like all hell had broken loose—people were yelling and Jeremiah thought he heard a shot, although nobody was in sight behind them and he didn't know what the hell anybody could be shooting at.

When they hit the sidewalk, both men slowed to a rapid walk. The vegetable market was crowded with morning shoppers, and it took several minutes for them to make their way through the store and out the rear door. It was then five blocks to the subway. Sirens were echoing behind them.

Jeremiah knew that for the rest of his life—however long that might be, given the present circumstances—he would never forget that subway ride back to Manhattan. They sat jammed together in a rear seat on the crowded train, not talking, like two strangers forced together by the vagaries of city life. Across the aisle a young black man dressed like a stockbroker read *The Wall Street Journal*. A boy with pink hair and safety pins in his ears stared at them, but it didn't seem as if he were really seeing them at all. A drunk dozed, and a bored cop stood at the far end of the car.

It all reminded Jeremiah of the time he accidentally wandered into a movie that was all in Italian. He knew that things were going on, he could see the action, but he didn't have an idea in hell what was really happening.

Max had to nudge him twice when their final stop was reached. Jeremiah stumbled a little getting off the train, bumping into Max. They caught a cab right away. Still in silence, they rode to Max's.

Once there, Max locked the door securely behind them. "See how simple it is?" he said, turning to look at Jeremiah.

Jeremiah didn't say anything.

"I always like to toast a job well done." Max poured two stiff drinks, then walked over and handed him one. "Here's to success, kiddo. You did terrific."

He downed the whiskey in one gulp, then regretted it immediately as the liquor churned up inside his gut. For one more instant he stood where he was, then he ran for the can, slamming and locking the door before dropping to his knees in front of the toilet bowl.

The burning in his stomach shot up his gullet, and he lost the booze. And the breakfast and, it felt like, everything else he'd eaten for the last month or so. The racking heaves took complete control of his body as he retched again and again.

He didn't know how long it was he knelt there, or how many times Max had knocked on the door before the sound reached him. He didn't answer. Instead, he got shakily to his feet, flushed the toilet, then bent over the sink to splash cold water in his face. There was a bottle of Listerine on the shelf. He sloshed a healthy slug around in his mouth to get rid of the bad taste left there.

"Jeremiah, we can't talk through the damned door. Get the hell out here."

He buried his face in the thick Turkish towel. Now he had to grow up and face life, he thought. And maybe it was about fucking time.

Jeremiah opened the door and stepped out, passing Max and going to the couch. He sat in one corner.

Max had followed him. "I didn't know that icing Costa was going to hit you so hard."

"It's not that," he said. His voice came out raspy from a sore throat.

"I know it's not, kiddo." Max poured two more drinks, then joined him on the couch. "I think it's time we talked about this," he said. "Way past time."

Jeremiah picked up his glass and took a small sip. The liquor burned his raw throat, but perversely, he welcomed the pain. He set the glass down again. "Raphael Tadzio hired me to kill you," he said flatly, staring at the floor.

"I know that too."

His head jerked up and he stared at Max. "What do you mean? You know?"

"Well, not all the specifics, but enough to add two and two and come somewhere near four. I'm not an idiot, for chrissake."

Jeremiah picked up the glass again, and this time the sip he took was much larger. "How long have you known?"

"Pretty much since the first."

"Since the first," Jeremiah repeated dully. He felt as if someone had run him over with a truck. A big truck. "If that's true, then why the hell . . . ?" He couldn't find the words to ask what it was he wanted to know.

And Max apparently didn't have an answer for the unasked question. He just shrugged and drank a little, then said, "I don't know. Maybe because just once in my life I wanted to do something that wasn't part of the program. Maybe I was bored. Besides, you're such a dope sometimes that it was kind of fun watching you fall all over yourself."

"Thanks a lot."

"Mind one question from your intended victim?"

"What?"

"Why does Tadzio want me burned?"

Jeremiah was a little surprised. "Hell, I don't know. Don't you have any idea?"

Max shook his head. "Not at the moment. Excepting maybe that the man is a bigger jackass than I always thought he was."

"Hey, I'm the jackass he sent out to do the job, don't forget. So which one of us is dumber?"

Max set his glass down. "So what happens now?"

Jeremiah reached under the sweatshirt and took out the gun. Max just watched. "What happens next is that I don't kill you."

Max shook his head. "Dumb move, kiddo, really dumb. Tadzio is not going to like that."

"Fuck Tadzio."

"Tough talk. Stupid talk. You don't do this job, it's like hanging a target on your chest. A fucking red bull's-eye."

Jeremiah put the gun onto the table and pushed it away with the tip of one finger. "I don't care."

Max seemed to lose patience. "You damned well better start caring. Christ, every time I think you've been as dumb as you can get, you go one step further. Just what do you think is going on here, anyway? Fun and games? These men are serious, buddy boy, and they take their business seriously. Deadly seriously."

Jeremiah, bewildered, looked at him. "What's the matter? You sound like you want me to kill you."

Strangely, Max smiled. "That assumes you could."

"Well, it's all . . . irrelevant, anyway, because I'm not going to try."

"Okay," Max said with a shrug. "Fine. Dumb, but it's your choice."

Jeremiah leaned back against the couch, his eyes on Max. "We can do it, can't we?"

"Do what? And when the hell did this become 'we,' anyway?"

Jeremiah ignored the second question. "We can get through this mess, can't we?"

"You mean alive, I guess."

"Of course I mean fucking alive."

"Well, I don't know. I wouldn't put any money on our chances, if you want the truth. No big money, anyway. But I guess we'll find out."

Jeremiah was quiet for a moment, then he took a deep breath and exhaled slowly. "We can do it."

"You think so, huh? Well, that sure as hell puts my mind at ease."

For the first time in a long time Jeremiah smiled. "So look at it this way—are you bored?"

2

Aaron just kept shaking his head at the persistent minicam reporter who was throwing questions at him fast and hot. The killing of Nick "the Weasel" Costa, unlike the other three recent syndicate murders, had caught the fancy of the press. The reporter, who looked to him as if she should have been representing a high-school newspaper instead of one of the big three networks, trailed after him like a small redheaded bulldog.

But Aaron had been around too long to fall into the trap of chatting with the press. He smiled nicely and said not a thing.

Finally, she gave up, angrily signaling her cameraman to turn off the tape and saying something under her breath that only sailors used to say.

Aaron tsked-tsked her.

Cody was leaning against the car, watching the scene with undisguised amusement. He took the cigarette out of his mouth. "So we have another body," he said. "We have a gun with no prints. Not to mention a couple of very nice little bomb blasts, which is the touch I love the most. And it looks to me like the stakes are getting higher. Costa was no ordinary foot soldier; even I know that."

"No, Costa was a fucking big deal, all right." Aaron was quiet as they watched the bagged and tagged body being loaded into the meat wagon. Not far away, the bomb experts were poking through the remains of the car.

"Well?" Cody said finally.

"Well. Let's go to talk to the witnesses first."

"And second?"

"Second, we're going to pay a little visit to my old friend Max."

"Trueblood? You're thinking maybe he pulled this off?"

"I think." Aaron's gaze swept the park. "Of course, the damned blasts don't fit anything he's done before, and that puzzles me. But, yes, I think Marberg hired Max to eradicate Costa."

Cody looked a little skeptical, but he shrugged agreeably and got behind the wheel for the drive to the precinct house, where the old men who'd been playing boccie with the deceased were waiting.

It was late that afternoon before they made it to True- blood's. "Hope we're not too late," Cody said, parking illegally in front of the building and flipping the POLICE BUSINESS sign into place.

"Too late?"

"Maybe he split already."

"Why the devil would he do that? This is where Max lives. He's not going anywhere." Aaron climbed the stairs, followed by Cody, and knocked on the door. It took several moments and another knock before someone appeared. He was sur- prised to realize that the door had been opened not by Max, but by the same young man they'd seen with him before.

"What?" the stranger said.

"We'd like to see Max," Aaron replied pleasantly.

He glanced over his shoulder into the room. "Max?"

"Come on in, Aaron," they heard Trueblood say.

They followed the young man inside. Max was in the kitchen, stirring something that smelled strongly of garlic and oregano. "Have you folks met Mr. Donahue?" he said.

"Not yet," Aaron said.

That seemed to be all of the introduction they were going to get. Donahue perched on the back of the sofa, his arms crossed. Cody sat in a chair opposite him as Aaron walked on into the kitchen. "That smells good."

Max looked up. "Thanks. You just came over for dinner, is that it?"

"No. Actually, we came by to bring you some news."

"I didn't know that was part of your job." Max moved to the counter and began to chop some onion. "But I appreciate it."

"Costa was killed today."

"Old Nick the Weasel? Well, that's too bad. I guess."

"Now there's a question."

"Sure. There always seems to be a question."

"What were you doing today?"

"Me?" He tossed the pieces of onion into a skillet of melted butter, stirring them lightly as they sautéed. "Why would that be of any interest to the police?"

"The hit on Costa was very good. It was nearly perfect, in fact."

Max's smile was impossible to read. "Nearly?" he said mildly.

Cody looked up from his perusal of Max's tabletop cigarette lighter, which was made of silver. "Let's just say it had the touch of a master."

Donahue, who looked sort of washed-out and puffy-eyed, with a nice shiner to boot, nevertheless smiled. Close up, he looked like a guy who smiled a lot. "Haven't you heard?" he said. "Max is retired."

"So you must be his nurse, I guess," Cody said idly.

The dimple disappeared. "I'm just a friend."

"Uh-huh."

They stared at each other.

Aaron had listened to the exchange. "You getting sociable or what in your old age, Max?"

"Jeremiah likes my spaghetti sauce" was all Max said.

"Sometimes a man goes too far," Aaron said. "After forty years even you might get careless. Might push your luck too far."

"Anything is possible, I suppose." Max glanced at him. "What is it, Aaron? You trying to scare up one more big bust before they put you out to pasture with the rest of us?"

Cody stirred. "We're both on this case."

"Good. I like to see the cops doing their job."

Jeremiah Donahue snickered.

"One thing about the Costa hit," Aaron said. "Whoever did it also blew up a car and a fence. As far as I know, Max, you never fooled with that stuff before. Am I right?"

"Right. Bombs are not my style."

Aaron turned and stared at Donahue suddenly. "How about your friend here. What's his style?"

Max turned the flame down under the sauce. "Nice to see you, Aaron. And you, too, Blaine."

That seemed to be an end to it. Cody was obviously bothered by the fact that Max, rather than Aaron, seemed to be the one in charge of the conversation and the situation. But he just walked to the door with Aaron. Donahue followed them, maybe to be sure they were really leaving. He didn't smile or bid them a fond farewell. He just shut the door. Hard.

Cody tried one more time as they got out of the car. "Aaron, your daughter is going to be mad enough that you're late for this damned dinner. It isn't going to make her any happier when she finds out you've dragged me along."

Aaron's face took on an injured expression. "Am I dragging you? This doesn't look like dragging to me. I invited you, that's all."

They stopped just outside the door of the trendy West Village café. "That," Cody said, "is not the point. She'll still be mad."

"But you're missing my point."

"Which is what?"

"I don't care if she is mad. What I don't want is to have to listen to her bitch about it. And she won't do that with somebody else there." He smiled. "Understand?"

"I understand that my own partner is using me."

"What's a partner for?"

They went in, and a hostess pointed them toward the right

table. Everybody pretended not to notice what was obviously a large gun under Cody's thin jacket.

Cody had never seen Aaron's daughter, and he was surprised to find out how pretty she was. She and her husband—Ted, he said, shaking Cody's hand firmly—were obviously not thrilled to see him there. Everybody milled around uncomfortably while the waiter fetched an extra chair and place setting.

It was several minutes before they were all sitting and a round of drinks had been ordered. "We were about to give up on you, Dad," Susan said then.

"Sorry. We had a killing today. Somebody gunned down Nick Costa in a park."

"So you had to work overtime?"

"Part of the job."

Both Cody and Ted sat in silence during the conversation. Susan was smiling, but there was an edge in her voice; Cody could understand why Aaron, who, despite all of his years on the force had always struck him as mild-mannered, was intimidated.

"Well, thank God it's a job that you're almost done with."

Aaron didn't say anything to that; he picked up the just delivered drink and took a sizeable swallow.

Cody followed suit with his Perrier. "You know," he said, "Aaron is a damned good cop. I'm very lucky to be working with him."

Susan smiled at him. "Yes. But I'm sure you will agree that he's earned the right to rest now."

"I think," Cody said carefully, "that he's earned the right to do whatever the hell he wants."

Ted cleared his throat. "Susan wants the best for him. We're really looking forward to having him move in with us."

"I don't think I want to do that," Aaron said.

He might as well have dropped a bomb in the middle of the table. After the explosion of his words there was a deadly silence.

Susan, though, obviously had a tough center, not unlike her old man. She recovered first. "This is something we'll need to talk about, Dad. So many plans have already been made. But the time for talk is not when there's an outsider present. So let's just relax and have a nice dinner."

"We'll relax. We'll have dinner. But I don't promise to talk about it ever again. And, by the way, Cody isn't an outsider. He's my partner."

Her expression was bright. "And we're very glad to have him here."

Cody had never felt so unwelcome in his life.

3

The dinner was good, and Jeremiah surprised himself by eating several helpings and actually enjoying it. Maybe his damned gut was settling down. "How'd you learn to do that?" he asked, finishing the last slice of garlic bread.

"What?"

"Cook."

"It's not hard. I like to eat well, that's all." Max stood. "Know what I don't like, though?"

"What?"

"Cleaning up. Time to pay the piper. The mess is yours." Max went to sit in front of the television to watch the baseball game.

Jeremiah made a face, but he really didn't mind washing up. Beat eating out of a can. He wanted to ask Max about the visit from the two cops earlier, but he knew that the other man would either just brush it off or get mad, so he didn't say anything.

The phone rang suddenly, startling him into almost dropping a plate. Max answered it without getting up from his chair. "Trueblood," he said. Then he replaced the receiver.

"Who was it?" Jeremiah asked from the kitchen.

"Nobody. Hung up." Max turned back to the ballgame, but he looked preoccupied.

Jeremiah put the last of the dishes away quickly and walked into the livng room, wiping his hands on the edge of the borrowed sweatshirt. "What do you think?"

"I think the bums are gonna blow the pennant tonight," Max said.

"About the phone call, Max. About the phone call, not the fucking ballgame." Jeremiah sat.

"Oh, that." Max shrugged. "I think it was probably Tadzio's people checking to see if I was still amongst the living. To see if you had done the job they hired you to do."

"That's what I was afraid of." Jeremiah stared blindly at the game for a while. "Max, what're we gonna do?" he asked finally.

Max glanced over at him. "Hey, you're the bright boy with all the big ideas. You're the idiot who crossed Raphael Tadzio. What you do next is your problem. Me, I'm just going to sit here and watch the game, then maybe go down to the Dying Swan for a beer. You can join me, but I don't want to listen to your mouth flapping about poor us and what happens next."

Jeremiah opened his mouth and then closed it again without saying anything. This probably wasn't a good time to bug Max too much. The last thing he wanted right now was to find himself out there on the street all by himself, with Tadzio's apes on his heels.

He started to watch the game, secretly rooting against the Dodgers.

A couple beers too many earlier at the Dying Swan and now he was paying the price. Jeremiah rolled off the couch again and went into the john, being as quiet as he could in the process. There was no sense in making himself an unwelcome guest.

When he came back to the living room, he paused to look

out the window. The moonlight seemed extraordinarily silver. Thankfully, the street below was empty.

He dropped the blind back into place and returned to the couch. It was pretty comfortable; better, in fact, than his own lumpy bed back home. Still, he was having a hard time falling asleep. Too many possibilities, none of them very pleasant, kept coming into his mind.

Finally, he tightly squeezed his eyes closed and started counting sheep.

The crash of breaking glass that woke him from the restless sleep he'd finally fallen into was followed almost immediately by the dull thud of something heavy and metallic hitting the wooden floor.

He sat up. Just as he started to say something real clever, like "What the hell was that?" the whole room seemed to explode in a bright flash.

Jeremiah resisted the temptation to duck under the blanket. Instead, his ears still ringing from the blast, he jumped up, grabbing for his jeans. "Max, get the fuck out of here," he yelled, tugging and pulling the jeans on as he hopped and stumbled toward the door.

The heat from the spreading flames was starting to singe him. He was struck by a crazy thought: It was sort of interesting to be on this end of a bomb.

Max appeared suddenly. He had apparently taken the time to don pants and a T-shirt, or maybe he'd been sleeping in them. There were moccasins on his feet and a leather briefcase under one arm. "Move it, boy," he said hoarsely.

Jeremiah was trying to work the three locks on the door, his fingers shaking, his eyes watering from the smoke. Behind him, he could hear Max coughing as the thick gray cloud swirled around them.

Finally, he flung the door open and practically fell out onto the landing, followed by Max. They both hit the stairs at high speed. Jeremiah could see that a small crowd was already gathering on the sidewalk below. Where the hell had they come from at this hour?

Just as his bare feet hit the pavement a shot rang out.

He didn't actually hear the report of a gun, but he knew that something whistled past his head, too close for comfort. Before his mind had quite accepted that, Max shoved him roughly. "Take off," Max said.

Jeremiah turned questioningly, but then another shot hit the wall beside him. He ran.

He could hear the people shouting and the wail of fire engines, but he didn't stop running until he was over seven blocks away. Finally, his lungs aching, he ducked into an alley and bent over, leaning against the building as he tried to catch his breath. There was a terrific cramp in his left side, and he rubbed at that before looking up.

Somehow he'd had the feeling that Max was still behind him. It wasn't until he quickly, unbelievingly, scanned the length of the alley that he realized he was completely alone.

Alone. In the middle of the fucking night in this city. No shirt, no shoes, just a few bucks in the pocket of his jeans, not even his wallet, which had been resting on the coffee table and was more than likely just a pile of ashes.

A great situation in which to find himself.

And all of that didn't even take into consideration the fact that there were people out here who seemed to want him dead.

Things had been better in his life.

He moved out of the alley and sat on the curb. Maybe he'd get lucky and a speeding cab would run him over. He almost laughed.

A couple hookers were walking by, on their way home, probably, after a night of work. They swung wide to avoid him, but he stood, trying not to look like just another New York crazy. "Hey, you don't happen to have a spare cigarette, do you, girls?" he asked, figuring that nobody with half a heart could resist such a wretched creature.

One of the women took out a cigarette and a book of matches. "Keep the matches," she said.

He nodded his thanks.

Somehow his dreams for the future had never included the picture of himself begging for smokes from a couple of whores.

This time he did laugh.

two:
no pain, no gain

1

After so many years on the job Aaron could wake enough to answer the phone almost before the first ring had faded. It didn't really matter much, of course, because there wasn't ever anybody else to be bothered by the sound. He picked up the receiver and listened to the voice of the night-watch commander but didn't saying anything except "Okay" when the message was finished.

He lay in the bed for two more minutes, waking up, then crawled out. It wasn't quite dawn yet, so he turned on a single lamp as he selected a pearl-gray suit, white shirt, and narrow black tie. As he shaved and dressed, he drank a cup of instant coffee made with tap water.

The sky was just beginning to lighten as he drove through the mostly empty streets to Cody's. He hadn't called before leaving, deciding to give his partner a little extra sleep. Blaine was inclined toward surliness if he didn't log enough sack time, but Aaron figured it was a trait he'd outgrow.

Although he'd dropped Cody off several times, he'd never actually gone into the building. The lobby had nothing in it but an old couch, which was occupied at the moment by a teenage boy wearing jeans and a rock music T-shirt. He was curled up, sound asleep.

Aaron stopped beside the couch and nudged the sleeping boy with his knee. "Wake up, sunshine," he said.

The kid rolled over and blinked up at him. For that instant he looked about six, like any little boy waking up. Then he blinked again and the curtain descended. "Fuck off, old man," he said.

"I'm not an old man," Aaron said. "I'm an old cop."

"Shit," the boy said, sitting up. "All right, I'm leaving."

"You got a home?"

"Sure I do. But I'm having the place done over, you know, and the smell of wet paint makes me puke. So I can't go back for a few days."

Aaron shook his head. "Hell with it," he said. "Go back to sleep."

The kid grunted in what was probably supposed to be an expression of gratitude and settled down again.

Aaron rode the elevator to the third floor. It took several knocks before the door was opened to the length of the chain. "Yes?" the woman said.

"I'm Aaron Temple. I need to see Cody."

"Uh-huh." The door closed briefly, then opened all the way. A slender blond woman stood there. She was wearing a man's white shirt and very little else. Aaron kept his gaze directed at a point just beyond her shoulder. "He's on his way," she said sleepily.

They stood where they were, not saying anything else, until finally Cody wandered in, shaking his head in an apparent attempt to get the blood circulating through his brain. "Aaron? What's going on?"

"Somebody firebombed Trueblood's place."

That seemed to wake him up quickly. "No shit?"

Aaron nodded.

Cody spun around and headed back for the bedroom. "Ready in five."

Actually, it was only about four minutes later when he appeared again, wearing painter's pants and a black T-shirt. He grabbed his holster from a doorknob and smiled brightly. "Ready."

The boy was sound asleep again when they passed through the lobby. Cody didn't seem to notice him.

By the time they reached the scene in Soho, the fire was out and the spectators had vanished. Only a single squad car was still on the scene, along with one hook and ladder that was about to depart and another car that was probably from the fire inspector's office.

As Aaron and Cody stood on the sidewalk, a man got out of the car and walked over to them. "Duncan, Arson Squad," he said. Then, with a wave at the building, "What a mess, huh?"

That was a fact.

Aaron stared at the gutted remains of the building; the explosion and flames had done their work well. Very little was left of either the loft apartment or the art gallery below. He shook his head. "Anybody inside?"

"We didn't find anything. Witnesses reported seeing two men run out of the place just after the fire started."

"Trueblood and Donahue?" Cody said.

"Probably. So they got out."

"Right," Duncan said. "The funny thing is, the witnesses also claim that there were shots fired at the two men as they escaped."

"I'm sure there were." Aaron walked a little closer and peered into the remains, wondering about the poor slob who had owned the gallery. What would he do now? "And so, what happened to the men?"

Duncan shrugged. "Disappeared."

"If they were smart," Aaron said.

Cody kicked at a chunk of charred wood. "What do you think, Aaron? Somebody looking for revenge for the Costa hit?"

"Could be, I guess." But Aaron frowned. "It doesn't feel right, though."

Duncan glanced at his watch. "If you two don't have any more questions . . . ?"

"No, take off. We'll wait for the report."

"Won't tell you much you don't already know. Somebody threw a bomb and burned the building."

"Thanks."

Duncan got into his car and drove off in the wake of the fire truck.

"Maybe somebody just doesn't want to have Trueblood back in action again."

"Maybe. We'll ask Max when we find him."

"If the other guys don't find them first," Cody pointed out.

"Well, Max is a survivor. If I were a betting man, I'd be willing to lay down a little on him."

Cody looked at him, doing a bad job of stifling a smile. "Aaron, I had no idea you were such a fucking sentimentalist. It almost sounds to me like you're rooting for that killer."

"I'm not 'rooting' for anybody, as you put it."

"Right. You're just relentless in the pursuit of justice, I guess."

"What I am is ready for breakfast."

"And then?"

"I don't know yet. Maybe we'll look for Max. Or maybe I'll just let you take over."

"That'll be the day," Cody muttered as they started for the car.

2

He had taken a very roundabout journey.

Max half jogged and half walked until he was five blocks away from the burning building and the gunshots. He stepped into a doorway to consider the situation. It was a little sticky, but he was reassured by the usual incompetence displayed by the creeps sent to eradicate him. Those dopes couldn't kill a fly with a swatter and a can of Raid.

Still thinking, he took out a cigarette and lit it.

Of course, there was still the possibility that even those dopes could manage to ice somebody even dumber. So maybe they'd gotten lucky and scored one out of two. The last he'd seen of Donahue, the kid had been hoofing it away pretty fast, but Max hadn't lingered long enough to see what had happened next.

It would be too bad if Jeremiah was dead, but, Christ, he was so damned stupid. Max shook his head. *I should've gotten a dog,* he thought, *if what I wanted was fucking company.*

He heard a car approaching and took a quick look. A cab— great, just what he needed. He flagged it down and told the driver to take him to Grand Central Station. From there he walked to the subway. One more short cab ride and then a two-block walk brought him to the apartment building where Jeremiah lived.

He tapped on the door several times, on the chance that Donahue might have already arrived, but when there was no answer, he sighed and used a credit card on the pathetic excuse for a lock.

The room was dark and empty.

So where the hell was Donahue?

Max turned on the lamp, then helped himself to a no-name beer from the small fridge. He took a gulp, grimacing at the taste. He would give the kid a couple of hours to show up, but that was all. This place might be next on the list, and Max had no intention of sticking around long enough to face the threat of being torched again.

So, a couple hours, tops. Which was more than he owed Donahue, but what the hell. Maybe he did bear some kind of responsibility for this; he could have gotten Donahue out of the picture a long time ago, instead of playing out the game.

He wandered around the room, studying the posters on the wall and the large collection of records. So Donahue was a music lover. Well, sort of, he amended, realizing that all of the albums were sixties rock 'n' roll. Well, at least it wasn't the heavy-metal garbage.

The soft tap at the door stopped Max's survey of the records.

"Jerry?" A whisper came from the hall. "Jerry?"

Max set the beer down carefully. He opened the briefcase, pulled out the .357, and walked over to the door. Instead of speaking, he just yanked it open.

The girl standing there looked startled, although less so than one might have expected someone to be under the circumstances. "Hey," she said indignantly. "What the hell are you doing in Jerry's apartment?" Then she apparently noticed the gun for the first time, because her face froze for an instant. "Jesus. Where's Jerry?"

Max didn't lower the gun. "Jeremiah's not here right now."

Her suspicious and spaced-out gaze raked him. "So who are you, anyway?"

"I'm nobody. Just a friend of his."

"Jerry never had any friends."

"So now he does. Me. And I'm just waiting for him to get home."

"Why the gun?"

"It's a dangerous city."

She seemed to take that remark to heart, nodding and biting her lower lip. "You gonna hurt Jerry?"

Jesus. "I said I'm a friend."

She looked around behind him, as if to be sure that nothing untoward was going on in the room. "Well, I know Jerry pretty good. My name is Sandy. You tell him I was here."

"I will." Max let the barrel of the gun drop a little. "Why are you here, by the way? Strange time to come visiting."

"Sometimes I come by after work is all. I live upstairs. Jerry and I screw once in a while. I don't charge him, 'cause we're neighbors. So I just came by to see if he was like horny or anything."

That explanation was somewhat more detailed than Max actually needed or wanted to hear. "Okay," he said. "I'll tell him you were here."

She studied his face once more, maybe for the police report if something happened, then turned and ran up the stairs.

Max closed and locked the door again.

He picked up the can of beer and dropped wearily onto the couch. Thinking back over what had happened, he allowed himself, for the first time, to feel a brief but sharp pang of loss for his home and all the things there. A big part of his life was gone.

Well, there was absolutely nobody to blame but himself.

After all, a man who violated the most basic principles of his life—for no good reason that he could see—deserved whatever the hell happened to him.

Despite himself Max smiled a little. Maybe this whole thing was the result of encroaching senility, or maybe it had happened because of boredom. The reasons didn't matter much now. Although what did matter wasn't altogether clear at the moment.

He shook his head.

So where the hell was Jeremiah?

Max leaned back to wait.

There was a big black guy sitting across the aisle from him. He looked sort of like Mr. T might on a bad day, and he was staring at Jeremiah.

Jeremiah shifted a little in the seat, trying to keep his own gaze directed out the window. This was the fourth train he'd been on so far. He couldn't decide where to go or what to do.

He was scared.

Mostly he just wanted to disappear, but it was hard to be inconspicuous when all you had on was a pair of jeans. He would have sold his soul—whatever was left of it, at least—for another cigarette. *Maybe,* he thought, *I should bum one from the African ambassador there.*

The notion made him giggle.

Christ, he decided, I'm losing my fucking mind.

Good way out, maybe. Go crazy.

Instead, when the train stopped again, he got off, more out of habit than anything else. Only then did he realize that his meandering trip had brought him very close to home. He decided to go there. Why not?

He walked quickly, staying to the inside of the sidewalk and keeping his head bent. The few minutes it took seemed much longer, and he went into the building with a feeling of relief.

The door was locked, of course, and he didn't have the damned key. It was sitting next to his wallet. But as he fumbled uselessly with the knob the door suddenly opened. He jumped back, at first seeing only the gun that was pointed at his head.

After several breathless seconds he realized that it was Max standing there, and the sudden release of fear drained him. He slumped against the wall. "Jesus," he said. "I thought maybe you were dead or something."

"Not yet. It's about time you showed up," Max said irritably. "Get your ass in here."

They both went inside, Max taking the time to lock the door again, then dropping onto the lumpy sofa. "Goddamn," Jeremiah said. "I've been riding that fucking subway for hours."

"Why didn't you just come here?"

Hearing Max ask it like that, it seemed like the simple, logical thing to have done. Jeremiah shook his head. "I don't know. I couldn't think is all." He rubbed the worn nap on the arm of the couch. "This is so crazy, isn't it?"

Max got up long enough to get the last two beers, then he came back to the couch and fixed Jeremiah with a hard stare. "Well, we have to start thinking now, kiddo, and thinking fast."

"I know, I know." Jeremiah drank greedily, then lowered the can and looked at him. "Hell, Max, I'm sorry. About your place. It's my fault what happened."

Max shook his head. "Tadzio torched the building, not you."

"Yeah, but—"

"Look, Jeremiah," Max broke in. "We don't have time to play these games. You're sorry. I'm sorry as hell too. But for sure, Tadzio isn't sorry. All he is, is mad. Very, very mad. He still wants me dead, and now he wants you dead too. And I don't know about you, but I'm not ready to check out yet."

"Me, either."

"Okay. Then put the bullshit aside for a moment if you can, and let's talk about what to do next."

"Whatever you say." Jeremiah took another long drink of the beer. He felt a little better already. Hell, Max had survived this game for a hundred years or so. He must know all the tricks. "You're the boss, Max."

3

This early in the morning the squad room was a quiet place to be. Two men from the night shift were drinking coffee and playing cards as they waited to be relieved. Another detective sat in the corner trying to catch up on his report writing.

Cody came into the room and walked over to where he and Aaron had their desks pushed together. Aaron was reading a file, but he looked up at Cody's approach. "Where the hell have you been?"

"You wanted breakfast, right?" He held up the white sack. "Hope you can get into an Egg McMuffin. It was the fastest thing I could find."

"Whatever, whatever."

Cody sat, pulling two sandwiches and two plastic containers of orange juice from the bag. "So? You uncover anything?"

"Not yet." He tossed the file aside and took off his glasses. His eyes were bloodshot. "They're supposed to call back with an address for Max's little friend Donahue."

"So eat and wait for the call. No sense killing yourself."

A small smile flickered across Aaron's face. "That would be one way to screw the retirement board, wouldn't it?"

"Maybe. But it would also fuck me up, because my dress blues don't fit anymore, and I wouldn't want to have to spring for a new set for the funeral."

"God, but you're a sentimental fool."

Cody chewed diligently on the sandwich and shrugged.

Aaron snorted. "Look, a Beau Brummel like you doesn't belong in a uniform, anyway. Hell, I'd look down from St. Peter's side and not even recognize you. Wear the jeans. Wear the yellow T-shirt, because that's my favorite."

Cody, in the middle of swallowing, nearly choked on the muffin. "The commissioner would love that," he said when he could speak again. "Not to mention Captain Ravello."

Aaron finished the last bite of his breakfast and looked at him. "So? You want to play kissy-ass with the politicians? Or do you want to make your dead partner happy?"

Cody drank some juice, considering. "I'll wear the fucking yellow T-shirt," he said. "But what I want to know is, how come you're so sure you'll be looking down and not up?"

Aaron just smiled and reached for the phone that had started to ring. He jotted down something the voice on the other end said, then got to his feet slowly. "Now we know where Donahue lives," he said, picking up his glasses. "Let's go."

The morning traffic was starting to gather in the city as they headed for the address on Tenth Street, so it took them a little longer than it should have to get where they were going.

Not that it probably mattered much, anyway.

When there was no response to Cody's knocking or Aaron's announcement that they were cops, he signaled the younger man to kick the door open. "You know what that feels like when you're wearing tennis shoes?" Cody complained.

Two kicks did the job and they were in.

The room was empty.

Cody walked over to the table and felt the sides of a half-full coffee cup. "Cold. They've been gone awhile. Assuming they came here after the fire."

"I think they did." Aaron opened the closet. There were some empty spaces, and one of the drawers was open in the bureau. "Looks like somebody packed in a hurry."

"Yeah."

Aaron shut the drawer and shook his head. "Dammit. They're in big trouble and I hope they know it."

Cody glanced at him, more than a little bewildered by the tone in his partner's voice. "Hey, you sound worried about Trueblood and Donahue. They're the bad guys, remember?"

"I know that, dammit. But no matter who they are, they deserve to be busted, not blown away."

"Whatever," Cody mumbled, starting another tour of the small room.

Aaron walked over to the window and stared out. "This is a damned big city when you're trying to find someone, but when you're on the run from the kind of creeps they're running from, it can seem pretty small."

"I guess." Cody picked up one of the many albums stacked next to the cheap stereo. *The Beach Boys' Greatest Hits*. God, did that bring back memories. Then he tossed the record aside and followed Aaron out.

three:

put it to music
and see who dances

1

Jeremiah pried the plastic lid off of the Styrofoam cup and peered inside. "No cream?"

"In the bag."

He fumbled around amongst the paper napkins, packets of catsup, and the other souvenirs of Max's visit to the hamburger joint, and finally found the little container of fake cream.

The Lafayette Hotel didn't have room service. Or a coffee shop. Or even plumbing that worked very well. All the dump had going for it, in fact, was that there were four walls to hide within while they decided what their next move should be.

Jeremiah unwrapped the cheeseburger with the works. He took a bite and spoke through it. "Didja think of something?"

Max was eating, with little apparent enjoyment, a plain hamburger. "What?"

"Before you left, you said we needed to come up with an idea. So I was wondering if maybe you did?"

"Did you?"

"Nope." Jeremiah took a swipe at some catsup running

down his chin. "I might as well tell you, Max, that this whole thing is pretty much out of my depth."

Max washed the food down with some coffee. "No kidding? Out of your depth? A slam-bang hitter like you?"

"Oh, yeah, that's me. Slam-bang. Let me tell you, except for a couple of times that must have been flukes, I never fucking did anything, except hot-wire cars and peddle VCRs out of the back of a truck. I was good at that. Ran a few numbers." Jeremiah smiled faintly, shaking his head. "A real John-Fucking-Dillinger I am. Oh, I blew up some candy stores a couple times, too, just so the owners would know we meant business."

Max sampled a French fry. "If you don't mind me asking, how come Tadzio contracted you for this job? Given your somewhat limited track record, I mean."

"He liked the way I handled a couple jobs."

"Like the Alphonse thing?"

By this time Jeremiah was beyond being surprised by anything Max knew. "Yeah, Alphonse. And a shark named Ngo." The smile turned into a smirk. "But the main reason he gave it to me was because I asked him for it."

Max raised a brow. "Really?"

"Oh, not specifically," Jeremiah said quickly. "I mean, I never heard of you, so obviously I didn't go to Tadzio and say lemme off Max Trueblood. I just asked for a job. Something important so I could prove myself, move up the ladder."

"You never heard of me?" Max said. "Thought you were a fan."

"Well, that was sort of a . . . an exaggeration." Jeremiah looked at him. "Hell, I'm a fan now, if that counts."

"Not much. So you wanted an important job and he told you to kill me."

"That about sums it up. I wasn't even looking to be a triggerman."

"No?"

Jeremiah crumpled up the wrapping from his burger.

"Frankly, I sort of was thinking of something in the executive field."

Max stared at him and then shook his head.

"Well, hell, I was just tired of being mostly a two-bit nobody with a talent for turning cars and buildings into rubble. I'm not a kid anymore, for chrissake. And I didn't want to end my life as only another cog in the machine."

"So you were a cog with big plans, right?"

"Yeah, definitely." He looked around the dingy room. "I have to admit, buddy, that things are not turning out just the way I had thought they would."

Max crushed the rest of the trash and shoved it all into the sack. "Hindsight seems to indicate that it would have been much easier to just kill me the way you were supposed to."

Jeremiah found a quick grin somewhere. "Or have tried to, anyhow."

"Yes, or have tried to."

He shook his head. "No. No, that wouldn't have been easier at all. Not for me."

Max looked at him for a moment. "I hate to say this, boy, but I don't think you've got much of a future in the business."

"This is different than what I'm used to. Nobody gets hurt when I heist a car or run a few numbers."

"Yeah, well, this is the big league. And let's not forget that people sometimes do get hurt when you play your little games with firecrackers, right?"

"Well, yeah. Twice, like I said. But that was funny. It was like I didn't really hurt anybody. Because I wasn't there, you know? I was sort of separate from it."

"That's a subtle distinction that Alphonse and Ngo probably missed."

Jeremiah shrugged. "Probably. Anyway, as far as futures are concerned, ours looks a little limited, I'd say."

"You have a point, for once."

"So? Did you come up with an idea?"

"As a matter of fact, I did."

"Terrific."

"We're going to Long Island."

Jeremiah paused in the middle of finishing his coffee. "Long Island? Why the hell?"

"Because I have a house out there."

"I didn't know that."

"Among the vast number of things you don't know. It won't be safe for too long because other people will find out about it, but it will give us more time."

"Time for what?"

"Maybe just time alive, but that's better than nothing."

"I guess." Jeremiah sighed.

"You don't seem so happy about this. Maybe you have someplace you'd rather go? We're not joined at the hip, you know."

"I don't have any place else to go."

"Okay. So you want to come with me?"

He nodded.

"Fine. The only question now is one of transportation. I'd rather avoid the trains."

It was easy to see that nothing, even the threat of imminent extinction, could keep Donahue's spirits down for long. The old grin was turning on and off again regularly. It was a wonder his goddamned face didn't ache. The teeth gleamed now. "I steal cars, Max, remember?"

2

Sam Marberg was obviously not accustomed to having his brunch interrupted by a visit from a couple of the city's finest. He agreed to see them since they were there, but he didn't like it much. The big shot didn't seem to feel as if they were worth missing a bite over.

They had been ushered into a small sunny room at the back

of the house. Marberg was being served his meal by a tall, thin black man dressed like a butler.

Cody was hungry again, and he eyed the fluffy omelet and crisp bacon wistfully. But no invitation to pull up a chair and join in was forthcoming.

Aaron sat, anyway. "Sam," he said, "we've got a problem."

"Everybody's got problems, Temple. It's not my job to help you solve yours."

"I thought all of you guys were into playing the good citizen these days. Trying to clean up the old image."

Marberg shook his head at the butler's offer of more coffee. "Well, that depends. Maybe your problem is something simple, like you need some money for the Police Benevolent Fund. In which case I'll be glad to write a check. I'm always willing to give for the boys in blue."

Cody glared at him; but Marberg just took another forkful of eggs into his mouth.

Aaron smiled. "We'd appreciate a check, sure. But that's not why we're here. You had lunch recently with Max Trueblood."

"So? Is that something for the cops to be interested in? I also had lunch last week with a state senator. I eat lunch a lot."

"The lunch is just part of it. Things seem to be happening lately. Like the recent demise of Nicholas Costa."

"A tragedy for the family."

"Right."

"I sent flowers. Two hundred bucks' worth of flowers."

"You're a very generous man, Sam, I always said that." Aaron paused just for a moment, then said, "Last night somebody tried to fricassee Max Trueblood."

Cody could see somthing—surprise, maybe—flicker across Marberg's face. But it was gone so quickly that he couldn't be sure.

"That's peculiar" was all Marberg said, between bites. "Max is hardly in a position to create problems for anyone."

"Why?"

"Well, he's retired." Marberg made a face. "As he keeps saying."

"Yeah, that's what we thought, that he was out of the picture. But he did have lunch with you, and then Costa gets himself dead."

"Life is full of coincidences."

"Hmm," Aaron said. He picked up a croissant, broke off a piece, and tasted it. "Nice roll. You know a kid named Donahue?"

"Max's bodyguard?"

Cody looked startled. "His bodyguard?"

"Yeah. That's what Max said, anyway. Didn't make much sense to me, because the punk wasn't even carrying. Bodyguard? Unless maybe he's one of those karate experts or something."

"Maybe," Aaron said. "Who wanted Costa dead most?"

Marberg just shrugged. "We could play these games all day, Temple, if I didn't have other things to do."

"Okay, Marberg. But I'm disappointed that you're not being more cooperative." Aaron stood and they started to leave, then he paused. "But let me suggest something to you."

"What's that?"

"I suggest you should be careful, Sam. People are dying, and you know as well as I do that once that starts happening, there's no way of knowing where it'll end."

"Thank you for your concern."

Cody followed Aaron out.

The visit to Marberg's house set the tone for the rest of the day. If anybody in the whole damned city knew where Max Trueblood might be, no one was talking. In fact, they had a hard time finding anyone who would admit to knowing that the man even existed. The reluctance on the part of the street people to talk seemed to indicate that the subject of Trueblood was very hot. That didn't say good things about Max's future.

It was almost two hours past the time when their shift was supposed to have ended before they finally gave it up. Feeling like a couple of whipped dogs, they went around the corner to the bar, settling at their regular table.

By common consent, nothing was said until Aaron's beer and Cody's ginger ale were on the table in front of them. Aaron reached across and stole the basket of peanuts from the neighboring table. He ate one slowly. "My daughter's on my back again," he said. "She still thinks I'm going to move in with them."

"And what do you think?"

Aaron sipped his beer, nodded, then grimaced. "I think I'd rather have you shove flaming bamboo sticks under my fingernails."

Cody laughed softly.

Aaron sighed. "You know, crazy as it probably sounds to you, I can almost understand why good old Max broke out and did the Costa hit. Christ, he must have been bored out of his fucking skull."

"Yeah, you might have a point," Cody said.

Aaron shot him a glance. "I can tell that you're really interested in these geriatric problems. Just remember— someday you'll be old too. Then see who the fuck cares."

Cody set his drink down. "Dammit, Aaron, I care. Christ, I think it sucks. You think I like the idea that they're tossing my partner out?"

"Okay, okay. You care. Sorry. It's just that the thought of going to live with those people makes me crazy."

"So don't go."

"Sounds simple when you say it."

"Goddammit, Aaron, it *is* simple. Just fucking say no."

"I keep saying it, but I don't think anybody's listening."

"So say it louder and meaner. Aaron, I know you well enough to know that you never have a problem making people hear you when you want to. Don't start acting like you've lost it just because the assholes upstairs say you have."

"Maybe you've got something."

"Sure. I mean, I'd rather you stayed right here." He smiled slyly. "You could be like a silent partner. You know, sort of on call, whenever I need some fast advice."

Aaron looked disgusted. "Well, that sure as hell will give me a reason to keep on living."

Cody shook his head. "Aaron, you don't have to give up control of your life unless you fucking want to. You decide. Take charge, dammit, the way you always have."

Aaron just looked at him for a moment, then nodded.

He was unlocking his car when someone spoke from the shadows. "Evening, Temple."

He recognized the voice. "Thought you'd left town for good, Georgie."

"Yeah, but Chicago didn't agree with me. Too damned windy."

Aaron turned as the man shuffled toward him. George Lemat was a reasonably reliable snitch, when he was sober. About five feet tall and almost that wide as well, he seemed to own only one thing to wear, a dusty brown suit. Or maybe he had a different dusty brown suit for every day of the week. Aaron leaned against the car. "Too many Chicago bookies on your case?"

George coughed hugely and spit a wad of phlegm to the ground. "Ahh, you know how it goes."

"Uh-huh."

"I heard you been asking questions all day."

"I'm a cop, Georgie. Asking questions is how I earn my living, such as it is."

"Getting any answers?"

"Not many," he admitted. He took a stogie out of his pocket but didn't light it.

"If maybe somebody had something for you, what might it be worth?"

"That would depend on what somebody had."

Georgie produced another sizeable glob and arced it through the air. It landed with a plop. "Ahh, you're a Jew, all right, ain't you? Bargain, bargain."

Aaron didn't respond to that.

"Okay. As it happens, I've heard some things about a mutual acquaintance."

"Trueblood?"

"If you like. I found out who wants him dead."

"Who?"

"Tadzio."

"Why?"

Georgie didn't say anything.

Aaron sighed and took out his wallet. Tucked in a hidden pocket were two one-hundred-dollar bills. He took one out. "Why?"

"Poor old Tadzio has got a bad case of the scareds. Too many bosses going to jail. Too many people starting to expire unfortunately. Things have been very tense lately between Tadzio and some of the other bosses. Marberg, for example. He knew that Marberg was going to hit Costa, that he was going to try and get the best—Max—for the job, and he got scared that he might be next on the list. So he hired someone to hit Max first. You know those jerks; that's how they think."

"Yeah, I know. Who took the contract?"

"Don't know that," Georgie said with real regret; had he known, it would have been worth some more green.

Aaron handed him the folded bill. "This buys me some future consideration too," he said. "Anything else on this?"

"Tadzio is irked because the contractee ain't delivered as promised. That's why the fire at Max's."

"Okay, Georgie, thanks."

The short, fat man coughed his farewell and shuffled back into the shadows that seemed his natural habitat.

Aaron looked at the cigar, then stuck it back into his pocket and got into the car.

3

The crummy black-and-white television flickered and made an annoying buzzing sound as Max tried to watch the news. Jeremiah got tired of staring out the window and turned around. "Max, when the hell can we get out of this place?"

Max, who was stretched out on the bed, glanced at his watch. "I guess now is as good a time as any."

It was just after eleven, and after a whole day spent in the miserable room Jeremiah was more than ready to move. He was so ready, in fact, that he was starting to twitch.

In only five minutes they had vacated the premises, with no regrets. They walked four blocks through the relatively quiet streets—there wasn't much nightlife in this neighborhood, unless you counted the crime rate. Finally, Jeremiah spotted a car that he thought looked promising. He glanced around and liked the moment. "There she is," he said.

Max didn't even bother to look. He just strolled on, browsing in the barred windows of the closed businesses.

Jeremiah was into the Chevy and had it running in about forty-five seconds. He almost wished that it had been more of a challenge, so that he could have shown off a little to Max.

He glided the half a block to where Max was standing in front of a pawnshop. Max got in quickly and they pulled away from the curb. "You do that very well," Max said as they turned the corner.

"Thank you," Jeremiah said with uncharacteristic modesty that didn't ring quite true. "It's my best trick."

"You should have been happy just being a damned good car thief," Max said. "Life would have been easier."

"That's true, I guess," Jeremiah agreed glumly.

* * *

Jeremiah turned out to be a competent driver who didn't seem to enjoy conversation while he was behind the wheel, which was a nice surprise. Max watched the scenery flash by, also keeping a casual eye behind them. Nobody seemed to be following, but if they were good enough, even he might not be able to spot them.

They parked the stolen car in an empty lot behind a shopping mall, two towns away from their actual destination, then walked to an all-night diner from which Max called a cab.

Waiting for it to arrive, they sat at the counter and had some coffee. Jeremiah seemed to have gone into a slump, but Max was too tired to try to find out what was bothering him now. That was the trouble with having somebody around. You had to deal with them all the time. It was wearing on a man.

The cab finally pulled up out front and honked for them. It was still a twenty-minute ride to the house. Jeremiah pulled his bag out and stood on the curb as Max paid the driver. He seemed impressed beyond what the small bungalow deserved. "This is yours, huh?" he said as Max unlocked the door.

"All mine. Even the bank doesn't have a piece of it anymore."

"It must be great, having a house of your own. And this one is nice."

"Thanks."

Max was tired. After giving Jeremiah a brusque tour of the premises he went to take a shower. Sometimes standing under the hot water stream gave him good ideas, but all he got this time was clean. When he realized that he was in danger of falling asleep where he stood, Max got out. He dried himself briskly, pulled on some clean pajama bottoms, and went back to the living room.

Jeremiah was snoring on the couch, which should assure a great backache by morning. But Max left him where he was, tossing a blanket over him, and then went to bed himself.

four:

changing the rules
in the middle of the game

1

"He who hesitates is lost."

Max looked up from the book he wasn't really reading. "What did you say?"

"He who hesitates is lost," Jeremiah repeated.

"Oh, that's very good. You just make that up, did you?"

Jeremiah waved a hand in the direction of the large television screen. "That's the puzzle. I figured it out, and that dumb broad, who's some kind of teacher, didn't get it. I could've won the twenty-seven-foot yacht."

"Great. That's just what we need most right now." Max closed the book. "I thought maybe you had some line of action to suggest."

"Not me." Jeremiah jumped up and walked around the room again. He'd made a lot of trips around the furniture during the long day. "I'm hungry," he said, not for the first time.

"You know what's in the kitchen."

"Yeah. Seven cans of soup and a box of oatmeal." He stopped and pulled back the curtains to stare out the window. In just twenty-four hours the long summer had become fall. A brisk wind tossed gray clouds around the evening sky. "Is there a store close by where I could get us some real food?"

"Couple of miles that way," Max said, waving vaguely. He walked over to a drawer and took out a set of keys. "Car's in the garage."

Jeremiah caught the keys on the fly and started for the door. Then he paused. "Uh, Max . . ."

"What?"

"Tadzio never paid me for icing you, which I guess is okay, since I never did it, anyway. And you haven't given me my cut on the Costa job yet, either. So I'm broke."

Max reached for his wallet and counted out a hundred dollars. "This isn't part of your cut," he said. "This is expense money. You'll get your share, don't worry about it."

"I'm not worried. You have an honest face."

"Get enough stuff for a few days, just in case."

"Just in case?"

Max smiled a little. "Just in case we get lucky and nobody kills us immediately."

"You know, Max, it's hard not to love a guy with your sense of humor."

Jeremiah left before Max could respond to that.

The car turned out to be a new red Fiero, which startled Jeremiah a little because it didn't seem to be in character with what he knew about Max. But then maybe he didn't know as much as he thought.

He backed out carefully, aware that the owner was watching from the window. Then, unable to resist, he gunned the engine and squealed away.

Let the old bastard worry a little.

Jeremiah took his time over the shopping, pushing the cart up and down every aisle slowly, jostling with the housewives and trying not to run over the kids. Figuring they deserved a treat, he tossed a couple of thick steaks into the cart. After adding a six-pack of Pepsi and some Twinkies, he started for the checkout.

Although everything he'd bought fit into only two bags, it seemed to use up a lot of the hundred bucks, and he hoped that Max wouldn't be mad. But he seemed to toss money around. Probably he had plenty to toss.

He was bending to put the groceries into the car when the gun barrel was jammed unceremoniously into his spine. Surprisingly, he wasn't all that surprised. Maybe he'd been expecting something like this.

"You like walking around?" a low voice said.

Although it seemed like a rhetorical kind of question, he answered it, anyway. "Sure."

"So maybe if you do just like I say, you'll still be walking around when this is all over."

"Right."

"We're gonna go around to the back of the store."

"You're the boss." Jeremiah took a moment to lock the car.

They moved slowly, and during the whole journey, the gun stayed just where it was. There was a long black car parked at the far end of the rear lot. He couldn't see anything through the windows, but it made sense that Tadzio was sitting in the backseat when Jeremiah got in. The door closed, leaving them alone.

Nobody said anything for several minutes.

Tadzio finally sighed. "You've turned into a very big disappointment to me, Jerry," he said.

"I'm sorry about that."

"Are you? You're sorry? Is that supposed to matter? So Jerry is sorry. Does that make it better?"

Jeremiah shrugged.

"What happened to the boy with all the fancy talk?"

"What would you like me to say?"

"Maybe some reason for this? In good faith I gave you a job. And remember, please, how it was. You came to me, asking for a chance. Which I gave you."

"Yeah, I know that." Absurdly, Jeremiah found himself thinking about the fudge-ripple ice cream he'd bought, hoping that it wasn't melting all over the Fiero's upholstery. "Listen, Mr. Tadzio, the thing is, I just couldn't kill Trueblood. I met the guy, you know? I met the guy and I just couldn't kill him. You understand that?"

"The only thing I understand is that you betrayed my trust. That hurts."

"Yeah," Jeremiah said bitterly. "And without even trying to find out what was going on, you tried to burn my ass. That doesn't show much loyalty, either, if you want my opinion."

Tadzio seemed to concede him that point, and Jeremiah allowed a little hope to creep into his heart. Maybe this whole fuck-up wasn't beyond fixing.

"Maybe that action was a little . . . premature," Tadzio said.

"Maybe?"

"That depends on what happens next."

"Well, it seems to me that what happens next is pretty much in your hands," Jeremiah said. "Under the circumstances."

Tadzio smiled briefly. "That's the spirit I liked in you before. There could be a future for you with us, after all. I'm going to give you a chance to salvage this situation."

"Are you? Why?"

"For many reasons, none of which should concern you at all."

"Okay."

Tadzio took a moment to glance at his watch. "I'm going to give you twenty-four hours."

"To do what?" Jeremiah asked, although he was pretty sure he already knew.

"To complete the contract."

"Kill Max Trueblood," Jeremiah said flatly.

"Exactly. Do that and you'll still be paid as agreed. And as a bonus you'll get to live long enough to spend the money."

"Otherwise?"

Tadzio smiled again. "There is no otherwise. Not for Trueblood and not for you."

Jeremiah nodded. "I understand."

"I knew you were a smart boy, Jerry."

There seemed to be no signal given, at least none that Jeremiah was aware of, but the door opened again. He slid out and stood on the sidewalk, watching as the car glided away and disappeared into the night.

He made the drive back to the house much too fast, but luck was with him—for a change lately—and there weren't any cops along the route. Once there, he parked in the garage, grabbed the groceries, and hurried inside.

"Max," he called out, putting the bags on the kitchen counter, "we've got a problem."

He walked into the living room.

The house was empty.

Jeremiah could have searched through the rest of the rooms, but it wasn't necessary. There was a special feel to an empty place, and the bungalow had it. He stood in the middle of the living room, not sure what to do. Then he spotted the envelope that been carefully propped against the desk lamp. His name was block-printed on the front.

Reluctantly, he crossed the room and picked up the envelope. It wasn't sealed. Inside there was a note and a thick wad of bills. He dropped the money onto the desk and sat down before unfolding the sheet of paper.

The handwriting was small and neat. Methodical. He wrote like he killed, carefully and with precision. For some reason he read the note aloud, as if he were reciting for a tough teacher: "'I finally got an idea. Take this cash and the car and get the hell out of here. We'll both be better off. Take care, will you? And for chrissake, try to smarten up a little.'"

The message wasn't signed.

"Shit." Jeremiah crumpled the note in his fist. Still holding it, he leaned back in the chair and began to count the money. There was ten grand, more money than he'd ever had at one time in his life. He spread the bills out into a green fan. His cut, apparently. Big deal. Max gets two hundred and fifty grand and gives him a lousy ten. Fuck that. It was an insult, that's what it was.

Take the money.

Take the car.

And smarten up.

Well, one out of three wasn't bad. He should sure as hell get smart.

And so should that stupid, stubborn bastard Max True-blood. The only chance they had was to ride this out together. Didn't the old fool know that?

Jeremiah absently fingered the bills.

Before he could come up with a bright idea about what to do next—although his options seemed severely limited—the door bell rang. He hesitated, then decided, what the hell, how could things get any worse? He swept the money into the drawer with one hand, then went to see who was visiting.

It was those two cops, Temple and Blaine.

Jeremiah was beyond being surprised by anything. "Come on in," he said. Without waiting to see if they did, he turned around and went back into the living room. He dropped onto the couch.

They had, in fact, followed, pausing in the doorway of the room. "Max here?" Temple asked.

"Nope."

"You mind if we wait?"

He shrugged. "Do whatever you want; it's not my fucking house."

With a glance at one another they took the two chairs facing the couch. Blaine lit a cigarette.

Jeremiah realized that he was still holding the note. He

crumpled it again. "Maybe I should tell you, though, that it might be a very long wait."

"Why?" Blaine asked.

Jeremiah spoke to Temple. "Max took off."

They looked skeptical. "Did he?" Blaine asked.

"Uh-huh," Jeremiah said to the old cop. "And I don't think he's coming back, you know?"

Temple was fiddling with a cigar, as if he wanted to light it. Jeremiah leaned forward and tossed him a book of matches. "Thanks," he said, still not lighting the stogie. "Donahue, is there something going on here that we should know about?"

Jeremiah gave a short, harsh laugh that he could hardly recognize as his own. "Sir, if I knew what the fuck was going on, I might even fucking tell you. Does that give you an idea of what kind of fucking shape I'm in?"

"You don't have any idea where he might have gone?"

"No. He didn't take the car is all I know."

Blaine exhaled. "Maybe he called a cab?"

"For all I know, the bastard sprouted wings and flew away," Jeremiah snapped. "Isn't he the great Max Trueblood?"

Nobody said anything.

As Jeremiah looked at the old man he could see an idea form behind the glasses. Maybe Temple wasn't just a dumb cop, after all.

Temple stood suddenly. "Well, if Max has split, there's no sense in us hanging around, is there?" he said, obviously startling his partner.

"Like I said, do whatever you want."

They left.

Jeremiah went to the window and watched until the two men were in their car. Then he ran through the house and out the back door. He had a feeling that the old son of a bitch might know where Max was, and this could be his only chance at finding out.

"If it's not too much trouble," Cody said, "would you mind telling me what's going on?"

"Nothing very important. I just have an idea where we might find Max."

Cody nodded. "Okay. Fine. Mind one more question?"

"You'll never learn if you don't ask questions."

"Just why are we looking for Max, anyway? Not to bust him, that's for damned sure, because we don't have spit tying him to the Costa hit."

Aaron didn't answer for a moment; instead, he finally lit the cigar, using the matches that Donahue had given him. "You want the truth? I don't know why we're looking for him." He sighed and smoothed his thinning white hair. "Maybe those assholes upstairs are right. Maybe I am getting too senile to be a cop anymore."

"Stop talking like an idiot," Cody said sharply. "You must have a reason for wanting to find Trueblood, so we'll find him."

"Yeah," Aaron said, mostly to himself. "I must have a reason."

They rode in silence until they reached a turnoff about three miles from the house. "Right here," Aaron ordered, and the car turned sharply.

Cody parked on a graveled drive that looked out over the beach below. Even from where they were, they could see a solitary figure sitting on a large boulder, smoking and staring out over the water.

Aaron opened the car door. "You wait here," he said.

"Is that smart?"

He smiled. "Max Trueblood never killed anybody he wasn't paid to kill. Why would anybody pay him to off an old cop?"

"Okay," Cody said reluctantly. "But I'll be watching."

"That makes me feel better."

He got out of the car, slamming the door. It was a little treacherous making his way down the sandy incline with one bum leg, but he made it without the humiliation of falling. Max didn't seem to notice his approach, but that was probably deceptive, because as Aaron got closer, he could see that one hand was inside the jacket, no doubt holding a gun.

"How're you doing, Max?" Aaron said, trying to catch his breath.

Max turned his head. "I'm doing fine, thank you." The hand slipped out from under the jacket. "This is a little out of your territory, isn't it?"

"Yes. But since this is an absolutely unofficial visit, that probably doesn't matter much."

"Social call, you mean?"

"Something like that." Aaron shivered a little and turned up the collar on his suit jacket. "Damn, it's cold out here."

Max dropped his cigarette into the sand and crushed it out with his foot. "It's the dampness down here by the water. Gets into the bones. Especially bones that are . . . past their prime."

"A nice way to put it."

"Well, it's true. The damp doesn't bother the young so much."

"Does anything?"

Max smiled. "No, probably not."

Aaron studied the glowing tip of his cigar. "Sometimes, Max, I find myself wondering if I was ever that young. As young as Cody."

"You were. And I was. A long time ago."

"I guess." Aaron shook his head. "Who the hell thought it would all go by so fast?"

"All what?"

"Life. Just life."

Max put both hands inside his jacket pockets. "It's not over yet."

"Not quite."

"I've got some living to do yet, if you don't mind."

"I don't mind a bit," Aaron said. "But somebody else seems not to want you around anymore."

"You saw my place, I guess."

"We saw what was left of it."

Max grimaced. "I'm going to miss it." He paused, then said with deceptive mildness, "That bastard."

"Tadzio?"

He glanced at Aaron. "Always said you were a good cop."

"A good cop is usually a cop with good snitches."

Max smiled.

"He really wants you dead, you know."

"Sure. It's not the first time." Max shrugged. "Although it might be the last, I suppose. But I won't go down without a fight."

"No, you wouldn't, I guess."

"Nobody should."

Aaron thought about those words for several moments. Then he said, "It won't be just Tadzio, you know. If people get the idea you're spooked, the whole pack will be on you in a hurry. A scared beast is dangerous. Especially a scared beast who knows too much."

"True."

"Who's this Donahue, anyway?" Aaron asked.

"Oh, Jeremiah. He's . . . just a young man going nowhere fast. A punk with dreams of being more. But since he's also a complete fuck-up, that probably won't happen."

"I see."

"Jeremiah's okay," Max said after a moment. "He knows his business."

"Which is?"

Max only smiled.

"Maybe when we get older, we'll need a backup," Aaron suggested.

"Could be. That might be true."

Aaron chuckled. "He seemed a little upset, just now when we saw him."

"Yeah, I suppose. Hell, I should've gotten a dog, you know?"

They were both quiet, watching the water.

"So, Max, what's going to happen next?"

Max glanced at him with a certain amount of scorn apparent. "That's the kind of stupid question my friend Jeremiah keeps asking. Like I'm supposed to know everything." He shook his head.

"Well, I guess all I can say is, step carefully."

"Aaron, I'm a New Yorker sixty-five years. I always step carefully."

They both laughed, and then Aaron turned around and started back up the slope toward the car.

Max watched him go, shaking his head a little as the other man scrambled to maintain his footing on the sand. He heard a car door slam and the engine turn over with some reluctance, then after a moment the lights and the sound disappeared.

Just an instant later he heard another car door slam, and Jeremiah appeared, making his way down the incline. He was moving too fast and nearly fell. Max just shook his head again and turned to look at the waves once more.

Jeremiah stopped beside him. "That old cop, he knew just where to find you," he said.

"Aaron? Yes, he'd remember. This place, this stretch of sand was where I made my first hit. A long time ago. Before you were born."

"Here?" Jeremiah looked around as if he were seeing some damned historical monument.

"Yes. Used to be a house down here. Big place, built in the

twenties by a very rich man. It was like something out of Fitzgerald. You know Fitzgerald?"

"*Great Gatsby*, right?"

Max was a little surprised. "Right. Anyway, one night the man who owned the house had a party. I think it was to celebrate V-E Day or something. A very big deal, anyway, this party. Live music and everything."

"Gatsby," Jeremiah said again.

"Uh-huh. In the middle of the party, when the orchestra was playing 'In The Mood,' the very rich man stepped outside for a little air and I shot him. I got two grand for the job. In those days that seemed like a lot of money."

"Still does to some of us."

"I guess."

Jeremiah rubbed his hands together. "Chilly, isn't it?" He was quiet, then said, "See, the thing is, I don't think I'd be able to do that. I thought I could, but . . . no, probably not. I still say it's different than wiring a car. Maybe not to the dead men, like you said, but to me."

Max nodded. "You're right, I think. But, you know, that's nothing to be ashamed of."

"Maybe. But it makes me look like a real ass, under the circumstances."

"Nobody's looking but me."

"And you already knew I was a jackass, right?" Jeremiah kicked at the sand. "Max, I have to say something."

"What?"

He took a deep breath. "I think what you did really sucks."

"What did I do?"

"Splitting like that."

"Hell," Max said with a measure of indignation. "I left you money. The car. I figured you'd be halfway across fucking Pennsylvania by now."

"Fuck the money. And the car. You ran out."

"Hey, it was an idea, right? We needed one."

"Not that one. I thought we had a deal to fight this together. I thought we were maybe like friends or something."

Max looked at him but didn't say anything.

Jeremiah kicked at the sand again. "Okay," he said. "I know what you said about not having any friends. And I understand. But I honestly don't think that applies here. I think we're sort of stuck with each other, whether we like it or not. And for the record, I don't mind." He looked up and stared at Max. "I think that if we just, you know, hang tight, we can beat this."

"Is that what you think?"

Something in Max's tone seemed to take the steam out of Jeremiah's determination. He stepped backward. "Okay. Look, forget it. I'm pretty fucking stupid. I know that and you know it too. Don't you keep telling me? I guess maybe you have to look out for number one and so maybe skipping out was the smart thing to do. Sorry. The money's in the desk. Keep my damned cut. What I did was worth more than that, anyway." He took the car keys from his pocket and held them out. "I don't want your car."

Max didn't take the keys. Instead, he massaged his temples. "Christ Almighty, no wonder Phil Donahue spends so much time talking about inter-fucking-personal relationships. I've got a headache."

"I don't want your goddamned car," Jeremiah said, dangling the keys.

"Jeremiah, shut the hell up."

Surprisingly, he did.

"I didn't mean to . . . hurt your damned feelings or whatever the hell it is I seem to have done. I just thought . . . well, it doesn't matter now what I thought. If you want to hang together through this, we'll do it."

"Yeah, that's what I want."

Max shrugged. "Okay. What the hell." He pushed the hand holding the keys away. "You might as well drive us back."

They started up the incline, then Jeremiah stopped abruptly. "Oh, by the way, I saw Tadzio tonight."

"Great."

"He gave me twenty-four hours to kill you."

"I needed to hear that right now. Jesus H. Christ."

Jeremiah opened his mouth, probably to give an exact report on what Tadzio had said.

"Not now. Nothing else now, please," Max said.

Jeremiah kept quiet.

NOBODY EVER SAID IT WAS GOING TO BE SIMPLE

one:

every man has his price

1

Jeremiah took two more beers from the refrigerator and went back outside. From the deck he could look out over the backyard, which was edged by a tangled wall of shrubbery, and beyond that, down a sharp precipice, was the water. The smell of the ocean mingled now with the odor of burning beef.

It was too damned chilly out here for a barbecue, not even to mention the fact that in light of all their other problems, this didn't seem like a very bright thing to be doing, but they had sort of decided to stop worrying for the moment. Or, more specifically, Max had decided to stop worrying and had ordered Jeremiah to do the same.

Jeremiah was trying. "Steaks almost done?" he asked.

Max, who was tending the grill with an abstracted expression on his face, nodded, using one hand to wave away the smoke.

Jeremiah wondered if the other man was aware of the passing time. It was, in fact, some twenty-five hours and fifteen minutes since his conversation with Tadzio.

This was probably a real dumb move they were making here. The smart thing to have done was just split. Put as much

space between Tadzio and themselves as possible. That was
what he had suggested. But Max vetoed that idea, explaining
far into the previous night how the best thing for them to do
now was try to force some kind of action out of the other guys.
The situation, he'd said, was still fluid, whatever the hell that
meant. Jeremiah didn't want to ask, because he probably
wouldn't like the answer.

So, instead of burning the highways west, here they were,
having a picnic and freezing their balls off. And waiting.

He held up two plates as Max speared the slabs of charred
meat and a couple blackened potatoes. "You know," he said,
walking over to the small redwood picnic table and setting the
plates down, "life is funny."

Max looked up from his contemplation of the dying
charcoals. "What's that, another puzzle?"

"No, that was just . . . a thought, is all."

"My God, you're starting to think. Looking death in the
face does strange things to some people."

"You're very funny. You ever thought maybe of going on the
Letterman show?"

Two shots rang out. They came from somewhere in the
darkened yard. One shattered a beer bottle on the table,
about half an inch from Jeremiah's hand. He dropped to the
ground instantly, rolling under the table. "Max?"

Max was on the ground too. He said something, but
Jeremiah couldn't understand the muffled words. He knew
then, though, where the second bullet had hit.

More shots sounded, kicking up little bits of brick.

"You bastards!" he yelled. That did no good at all, of course,
but it made him feel a little better.

Jeremiah took a deep breath, held it for several seconds,
then expelled it in a whoosh. Then he started moving. He
crawled on his belly across the deck toward the grill, getting
close enough to shake Max's ankle with one hand. "Hey," he
whispered. "Hey."

The only response was a low moan.

Three or four shots cracked into the bricks around them. Jeremiah shielded his face against Max's leg. "Max," he said when it was quiet again. "Dammit, answer me." He scooted closer and took the gun from the holster under Max's arm. By that time he was expecting another barrage of bullets from the invaders, and he waited, bent over Max, until they came. When there was another pause, he fired off the rounds in the pistol as quickly as he could, using the first shot to destroy the light hanging above the patio. They were plunged into darkness, and he fired the rest of the shots blindly out toward the yard. Then he dropped the empty gun.

He got a hold on both of Max's arms and began to move, dragging the other man across the deck to the door. Finally, ignoring the next barrage of shots smacking into the house, he tugged and pushed until Max's inert form was inside.

Even then he didn't stop until they were halfway across the kitchen. A streaked trail of blood marked their path.

First things first. He grabbed the shotgun from the table where Max had put it earlier and blasted both barrels through the door. Just so the creeps out there would have something to think about for a few minutes while he took care of business.

Then he crawled back to Max, who hadn't moved at all. "Max," he said urgently. "Max, wake up."

There was no answer, and he looked pale, but at least he was breathing steadily. The blood was coming from his left side, and there seemed to be a lot of it. Jeremiah tried to clear his mind of everything else, including fear of imminent death, and think quickly. Finally, he yanked off his warm-up jacket and pressed the wadded garment against the wound. Pressed hard and held it there.

Maybe that would do some good, anyway.

But he couldn't spare the time to wait and see. The shooters outside might come walking in anytime. He crawled back to the table, where two more guns waited, both .357s. Silently apologizing to Max for some of his cracks earlier about the

Alamo, Jeremiah took one gun in each hand. He quickly stood and crossed the kitchen to the light switch. As he left the room he hit the switch.

Jeremiah walked straight through the house and out the front door. For just the barest instant he considered one possible action: He could get into the garage, into the Fiero, and be gone before the assholes around back knew what was happening. Yeah, he could do that, it was probably the smart thing to do, and funny as it was to think about, he figured that Max wouldn't blame him. Hell, the old bastard would probably congratulate him on finally, *finally*, wising up.

But his footsteps took him right past the garage door and on into the damned jungle that Max called a backyard. His old lady didn't raise any smart boys.

The dummies after them weren't geniuses, either, he realized, or they would have left someone in the front. Overconfidence probably killed them. Or just stupidity.

Jeremiah wiped at the sudden sheen of sweat that covered his face despite the cool night air. He tried to walk carefully, but there was still noise from the dying foliage under his feet. Maybe it seemed louder to him than anybody else, because nobody fired on him. A few more bullets did hit the windows of the house. Jesus, no wonder Marberg hired Max when he had a job to do, if these guys were typical of the talent available.

When Jeremiah saw the first shooter, it was a surprise. He hadn't realized how close he was. The man in the dark suit had a short rifle raised to his shoulder. He was watching the house, but at the last moment he must have heard something that warned him, because he started to turn. He never made it all the way around.

Jeremiah fired the gun in his right hand, the power of the recoil startling him more than a little. The man stepped backward, then fell.

Jeremiah moved closer and put another bullet into him, just to be sure.

"Ronnie?"

The hoarse call came from Jeremiah's right.

When Ronnie didn't respond, the other man was silent.

Jeremiah dropped the first gun and held the second with both hands as he moved toward the voice. He wasn't even aware of feeling any fear now. If he felt anything at all, it was a kind of cold anger.

There was a sound to his left suddenly. He spun in that direction, lifting the gun and firing as he did. Another shot sounded immediately after his, and the bullet grazed his arm. It stung, like an insect bite, and he could feel a warm trickle of blood. He noted that with dispassion, then dismissed it from his mind.

Hide-and-seek.

Ollie, ollie, oxen free.

A sound, like a footstep, reached him, and he flattened himself against a tree, not even breathing. The man who appeared, walking on tiptoe, was the same creep who had taken him in the parking lot the night before. Tadzio really needed some better soldiers.

He spotted Jeremiah at almost the same moment.

Two guns fired.

Max opened his eyes to darkness.

He couldn't remember getting from the deck to the kitchen floor. His left side was hurting, a dull, throbbing ache, but when he fumbled around with one hand and discovered the makeshift bandage, he stopped thinking about that.

What he really wanted to know was where the hell Donahue had gone to and what was happening.

Urgently, he checked the holster, found it empty, then felt the floor around himself. There was no weapon within reach. Whatever was happening, he couldn't face it unarmed. Slowly, painfully, he dragged himself across the floor to the cupboard beneath the sink. When he reached it, he took a moment to catch his breath, trying to ease the jab of pain in his side.

Finally, he reached out with one hand and pried the cupboard door open. The Smith & Wesson was on the inside of the door. He tugged at the heavy tape that was keeping it in place, and at last the pistol slipped into his hand.

Immediately, he felt better.

A wave of dizziness washed over him and he closed his eyes briefly. "Shit, Max," he said. "Don't fall apart now."

Summoning up what was about his last reserve of energy, he scooted closer to the cupboard until he could sit up, propped against the firm surface.

Two shots sounded outside.

"Great," he muttered.

Somebody was going to be coming through the door, and it was going to be soon. He used one knee to help steady the gun.

More shots.

Damn.

Max closed his eyes just for a moment.

Then, sometime later, he jerked them open as the sound of footsteps crossing the deck reached him. The gun wavered a little as he fought off dizziness again. A figure loomed up out of the dark, then the room was suddenly flooded with light.

"If you kill me now," Jeremiah said wearily, "I'm gonna be real pissed."

Max let the gun fall. "You," he said.

Jeremiah came over and crouched next to him. "Me," he agreed. He reached out to check the position of the bloody jacket. "You were ready for them, huh?"

"Sort of. What the hell happened out there?"

"I killed the bastards," Jeremiah said flatly, peering at the wound under the edge of the cloth.

"You did?"

"Yes. I shot one in the chest. Twice. The other one I shot in the head. Also twice. Whatever brains that dope had went flying." He made the recitation absently, his attention on the wound.

"Then?"

"Then I puked my guts out." It was nearly a challenge, the way he said it.

"Okay," Max said.

His fingers poked and probed. "I filled their pockets with some heavy rocks, dragged them to the edge, and dumped the bodies into the water. Figured that would give us a little time."

"Jesus," Max said. Then: "You surprise me."

"I surprise myself." Jeremiah sat back on his heels. "You need a doctor."

Max wanted to object—he hated hospitals and all that—but he knew from the way his side felt that there was no choice. So he just gave a half nod.

After a little thought that wrinkled his forehead Jeremiah pulled off his belt and slipped it around Max, buckling it firmly to hold the cloth in place. "This almost killed you," he said, seemingly more to himself than to Max. "A few inches more and it would have hit your heart."

Max couldn't think of anything profound to say in response to that, and he didn't feel like talking right then, anyway.

Jeremiah put both arms around him and hauled Max to his feet. "This is gonna be like a joint effort," he said as they both rested against the counter. "Okay, Max?"

Max made a sound that he hoped sounded like agreement.

"So here we go," Jeremiah said.

He half dragged, half carried Max out of the house to the garage. It was a slow and very unpleasant journey. Max bit his lip to keep from groaning at the pain as he was lowered and propelled into the passenger seat of the small red car. Should've bought something with some goddamned room, he told himself.

Jeremiah was bent over him. "Hey," he said.

"Huh?"

"Don't you do anything stupid, Max."

"Like?" Max managed to say.

"Like up and dying on me. Don't you do it."

"I won't." Max roused himself a little. "Go inside. Get the briefcase from my room."

"Not now, man."

"We aren't coming back once we leave," Max said. "Get the fucking case."

"Okay, okay," Jeremiah said. He patted Max on the arm, then ran inside the house.

Max wanted to wait until he got back, but suddenly everything went gray and then black.

2

It was only the second time in his life that Jeremiah had been inside a hospital. The first time was when he was fifteen and his mother was dying. It took two days for her to finish the job that she had been working on for as long as he could remember, and there was nobody then to wait with him, just as there was no one now.

So he did again what he had then: chain-smoked, thumbed through old magazines, and paced the hallways.

He couldn't help remembering the way his mother had looked when they took her into the room that she never came out of, until it was time for the short trip to the basement morgue. She had been pale, a little blue around the mouth, and her skin was clammy. He was glad when her cold hand was no longer gripping his arm.

Jeremiah hadn't been surprised by his mother's death. Life on the streets had taught him much earlier that junkies had a short life span. He couldn't even remember grieving all that much when she was gone. To him, his mother had been mostly a shadow. A shadow given to violent mood swings, one day sweetly generous with the little she had to give, and the next being abusive and frightening. Most of the time he had felt more like the parent than the child.

Max didn't look much better when the emergency room people got him onto the gurney and hustled him away.

Impatiently, he closed the six-month-old issue of *Family Circle* and pitched it across the room. He didn't want Max to die. It didn't seem fair.

Someone came into the room and he looked up hopefully. But it was only a young uniformed cop. Jeremiah rubbed his eyes wearily and wondered with part of his mind when cops, for chrissake, had started to look young to him.

"You Mr. Donahue?" the cop said, flipping open a notebook that he probably though made him look official.

"Yeah?" he replied, making it a question.

"The hospital reported that a shooting victim was brought in. That you brought him. A Max Trueblood?"

"Yeah," he said again. Talking to officers of the law was a skill taught early and often in his old neighborhood.

The cop straddled a chair. "You want to tell me what happened? For the official report?"

He thought quickly, then said, "It was an accident."

"Hmmm?" the cop said noncommittally.

"Yeah. An accident." Jeremiah warmed to the tale. "Max was . . . he was like cleaning the damned gun and it went off. Scared the shit out of me, I'm telling you." That much, at least, was true.

"That's all there is?"

"Isn't it enough?" Jeremiah toyed with the zipper of his Windbreaker, which he had grabbed before leaving the house. It covered up the bloody shirt.

The cop chewed on the eraser end of the pencil. "Were there any other witnesses?"

"No. Just Max and me."

"And you are?"

"I am?"

"I know your name. But what's the relationship?"

"Friends."

He wrote something down. "This gun—does he have a license for it?"

"Oh, sure," Jeremiah lied. "I would guess so."

The cop nodded and shut the notebook. "I'll check that out in the morning. And I'll have to talk to Mr. Trueblood, of course, get his version of the shooting."

"No problem. When he's feeling better, right?"

The cop reached into his pocket and pulled out a card. "Have him call headquarters tomorrow, please."

Jeremiah took the card. "Sure thing."

When he was alone again, he lit still another cigarette. Had he handled that right? If not, Max would probably get mad. He only hoped that Max would be around to get mad. Anger he could deal with.

As he was crushing out the butt a nurse stepped into the room. "Mr. Donahue?"

He looked at her, trying to read something in the bland expression.

"You can see the patient now."

Jeremiah took a deep breath. They wouldn't be letting him in if things were too bad. Would they?

And, in fact, Max was sitting up in the bed when Jeremiah walked into the room. There was a heavy bandage on his side and he was pale, but otherwise he looked okay. "Hiya, kiddo," he said in a somewhat faint, but still recognizable, voice.

Jeremiah walked over to the bed. There were no tubes or needles in sight. "You okay?"

"Yeah. Looked worse than it was. All the bullet hit was flesh. But I might've bled to death without your help. So thanks."

He shrugged.

"Maybe there's hope for you, after all."

"Maybe so."

They were both silent for a long minute.

Max said finally, "I have to get out of here."

Jeremiah frowned. "That's probably not a good idea. Smarter to stay here and—"

"Buddy boy," Max broke in. "If I were smart, would I be here in the first place?"

"You have a point," Jeremiah said, smiling a little now. .

It took some fast talking to the doctor and a little arguing with him as well, but finally the discharge papers were signed. A wheelchair appeared, and despite Max's vocal opposition, he was deposited into it for the trip to the front door. Jeremiah was waiting there with the car. He got out to help, but Max shook off his hands and leaned back against the seat with a sigh. "I don't remember it hurting quite so much the last time."

"You've been shot before?" Jeremiah said, getting behind the wheel again.

"Once or twice."

Jeremiah just shook his head. He drove until they spotted a place to buy a six-pack. With that they headed down to the beach, though far from the house, and parked. Clouds moved rapidly across the moon, making shadows in the pale light.

Max took a careful sip of the beer. "So you killed Tadzio's boys."

"Yeah, I did that."

"And hid the bodies."

"Sort of."

"So maybe we have a little time. But not much." He smiled wryly. "We wanted to get things moving, and I guess we did." He drank again, thoughtfully. "Okay," he said finally. "We're getting out of here."

"Where are we going?"

"To the place where all the bad guys go sooner or later. Miami. Ever been?"

"Nope." He fingered the flip top. "But aren't we likely to see some people there we'd rather not see?"

"Probably. But I have a plan."

"Oh, good. I was afraid maybe you were counting on me to come up with something."

Max shook his head. "You've done enough for one day. Tomorrow we drive into the city and get some things I need. Then we head south."

"Okay."

Max looked at him. "You're just as agreeable as ever, aren't you?"

Jeremiah's only response was to reach for two more beers.

They decided to spend what was left of the night at the Thrifty Motel. Jeremiah again zipped up the Windbreaker to hide the blood before going into the office. "I'm ruining a lot of clothes on this gig," he complained before getting out of the car to check them in.

Max didn't say anything. He watched through the window as Jeremiah sweet-talked the elderly desk clerk out of her irritation at being awakened. In his drugged-up state Max decided that it was too bad Tadzio wasn't a broad, because Donahue could charm his way out of this with a woman. Or a guy who went that way.

He laughed a little, then regretted it.

Jeremiah slid back into the car, holding a key in one hand. "You okay?"

"Fine, fine," he said impatiently.

The car glided around to the side of the building, to a parking stall well hidden from the road. Luckily the room was on the ground floor, because he felt sure that any attempt to climb the stairs would have finished him off once and for all.

The only luggage they had was the briefcase, and since all that contained was some money, two guns, and a key, it didn't take them long to settle into the room.

The room itself was not worth noticing, so it was a good thing they were both too tired to give a damn. Jeremiah helped Max out of his bloody clothes and into one of the beds. Then he undressed and stretched out on the other.

"Jesus," Jeremiah said out of the darkness. "I'll never be able to sleep. My nerves are shot to hell and back."

It was less than five minutes later when Max heard the sound of snoring from two feet away. No doubt it helped to be young.

And stupid.

two:

---

taking the act on the road

1

Max woke up hours later, feeling, for a change, like a man his age. He rolled over in the bed, grimacing at the stab of pain caused by the sudden movement, and tried to focus his eyes.

Jeremiah was sitting by the window, drinking a can of root beer and watching the traffic through a hole in the curtain. "Time?" Max said through a dry throat.

"Almost nine," Jeremiah answered. He stood and walked over to the bed, handing him the soda can.

Max took a deep gulp before speaking again. "Damn, we have to get moving."

"Can you?"

"I can do whatever I have to." He sat up tentatively and was pleased to discover that it only hurt about half as much as he'd thought it would. "Call the airport and see what time we can get a flight out."

"We still going into the city first?"

"Yes."

He wasn't in the mood for any long explanations. Instead, he got up from the bed with a minimum of groaning and headed for the bathroom. Maybe a shower would help him get rid of the thickheaded feeling.

It did help, at least a little. He was just getting out when he heard the voice on the other side of the door. "You keeping that damned bandage dry like the doctor said?"

He touched it. "Mostly."

"Great."

He slipped into his pants and opened the door. "Take it easy, Mother. You call like I told you to?"

"Yes. There's a flight at eight-thirty. That okay? She said there'd be seats."

"Fine, yeah." He picked up his discarded shirt and made a face. "Neither of us can go very far in these clothes. First thing is, find a store and buy us enough things for a couple of days."

They spotted a big discount store about five minutes after leaving the motel. Jeremiah parked in the middle of the crowded lot and went inside, leaving Max to drink his McDonald's coffee.

He picked out four shirts—three were vivid Hawaiian prints, which he figured would be good for Miami, and one was plain white with long sleeves, in case Max wanted to be conservative—two pairs of plain khaki pants as ordered, and two pairs of jeans for himself. Moving more quickly once the tough decisions were out of the way, he quickly added underwear and socks to the shopping cart and, as an afterthought, a pair of swimming trunks just in case. Finishing off with a electric razor that would work off the car cigarette lighter, toothbrushes and toothpaste, and a comb, he headed for the checkout. On the way he picked up a cheap overnight case and tossed everything but two of the shirts and the razor into it.

They stood beside the car and changed shirts, although Max didn't seem real thrilled with palm trees and parrots. He reached out with one hand suddenly and touched Jeremiah's bare arm. "What's that?"

Jeremiah glanced at the angry red welt that he'd forgotten about. "Oh, nothing. One of the bastards last night got lucky is all."

"Why the hell didn't you say something about it at the hospital?"

"I forgot." He buttoned the shirt quickly. "It's nothing."

"Tell me that when your arm turns green and falls off."

Jeremiah shoved the overnight bag into the car. "We going into the city or not?"

"We are."

Jeremiah manuvered the car with ease through the heavy midtown traffic. Of course, he probably had a lot of experience, losing cops and the like. It seemed like their lucky day: there was even a parking spot not far from their destination, which was a bank on Fifth.

Max's side was throbbing by the time they had crossed the vast lobby and walked up the wide, curved marble staircase. He stopped for a minute to catch his breath.

"You all right?" Jeremiah asked softly.

"Fine. And if you ask me that one more time, I'll break your arm, okay?" Max exhaled and started down the corridor.

They were greeted at the far end by a uniformed guard. Max presented the safe-deposit box key and signed his name on the sheet pushed toward him.

The guard glanced at Jeremiah. "He going in too?"

"Yes."

The clipboard was pushed at Jeremiah and he signed as well.

They followed the fat guard to the inner room. "You wanna be alone?"

"Yes," Max said again.

The small wooden cubicle was about the size of a phone booth, but they both managed to get inside. Max sat on the wooden stool while Jeremiah stood behind him. When they were more or less comfortable, Max raised the lid on the box.

He lifted out four thick stacks of bills, leaving at least that many still inside the box.

"Jesus, Mary, and Joseph," Jeremiah said. "You're a fucking millionaire."

"Not quite."

"Close enough. Wouldn't you like to adopt me or something?"

"Shit." Max handed the stacks of money to him. "Put these away."

"Sure thing." He dropped the bills into the briefcase.

Max reached into the box again, this time coming up with a thin black ledger.

"What's that?"

A faint smile flickered across Max's face. "Our insurance policy. Maybe."

"Maybe?" Jeremiah took the ledger from him, but before dropping it into the briefcase with the money, he opened it and thumbed some of the pages.

Most of them were written on, in various colors of ink and with various dates, but all in the same small, neat hand that he recognized as Max's. "Is this what I think it is?"

Mac closed the safe-deposit box. "That's depends on what you think it is."

"A record, right?"

"I guess you could call it that."

"Jesus." Jeremiah put the book away quickly now, as if just holding it made him nervous.

Max leaned against the wall just for a moment, then he straightened. "Let's get out of here."

Jeremiah looked at him with obvious concern but, wisely, didn't ask if he was okay.

Since they had several hours to kill before it would be time for their flight, and since they didn't particularly want to spend that time on the streets, they checked into the Howard Johnson's on Eighth Avenue and Fifty-first Street to wait.

Max sat on the bed and started to make some phone calls, apparently trying to track down somebody named Angie, for purposes he did not seem inclined to share. While he did that Jeremiah amused himself by counting the money.

An hour passed quietly, and finally Max reached the guy he was looking for. "This is Trueblood," he said. "Yeah, yeah, I'm sure you've heard a lot. Don't believe all of it." Max leaned back against the headboard, one hand rubbing his side. "I need you should do something for me."

Jeremiah stopped fooling with the stacks of bills to listen.

"If anybody asks about me, I'm in Miami. Donahue is with me."

Jeremiah grimaced.

"And, Angie, tell them we got something with us. A little black book." Max listened for a moment, then smiled at something Angie must have said. "Yes," he said then, "I think you could say it might make very interesting reading for some people. It's like a diary of the last forty years. Names, dates, a whole bunch of nasty details. Just pass the word, okay?"

A moment later he hung up, apparently satisfied.

Jeremiah abandoned the money on the table and came over to sit on the bed with him. "Was that a good idea?"

Max shrugged. "I think so. Maybe not. Hell, let's call it a calculated risk."

"Okay," Jeremiah said, but he wasn't so sure it was okay at all.

"You don't like it?" Max asked.

Jeremiah shrugged. "What the hell do I know?" He stood again. "I'm hungry. Think I'll go down to the coffee shop and get some lunch. You think that would be all right?"

"I think it would be fine."

"You want I should bring you something?"

Max shook his head. "All I want is a little peace and quiet," he said. "Like an old man who's retired should have."

Jeremiah paused, smiling. "You used to have that. But honestly, were you a happy man?"

Max closed his eyes. "Get out of here."

Before he left, Jeremiah turned off the lamp and pulled the window shade down, darkening the room. He closed the door quietly.

The coffee shop was in the middle of an afternoon lull, so he had no trouble getting a table. He took one way in the back, trying to keep out of the line of sight of passersby. He ordered a hot roast beef sandwich and a chocolate shake. The food arrived quickly and he ate the same way.

"Jerry!"

He froze in the middle of a bite and looked up. "Sandy," he said after several seconds. "Hi."

She sat down across from him. "Where the hell have you been? There's been all sorts of strange people hanging around your place. Cops, even."

He finished the mashed potatoes. "Yeah, well, things have been a little dicey. But it's working out."

She was eating a Hershey bar and looking strung-out. "You know what somebody told me? Somebody on the street told me you were dead."

"Well, I'm not."

"Yeah, he said you were. Dead. But then he laughed and said you were a dead man, even if you didn't know it yet. Weird."

"Yeah, weird." The sandwich was starting to turn solid in his gut. He stood. "I gotta go, Sandy."

"When you coming home?"

He was counting out money to pay for the meal. "Never," he said, acknowledging that fact to himself for the first time. "Never, I'd say."

Her eyes darted from side to side. "So what about all your stuff, then?"

"You can have it. Sell it if you want to."

"Even the records?"

He ducked his head quickly, pretending to figure the check

again. He blinked a couple of times. "Yeah, even the goddamned records." Maybe, after all, it was only fair. Max had lost everything, so why should he come out any luckier? He'd miss the records, though.

They said a fast good-bye—he was eager to get back to the safety of the room, and she was already adding up her profits—and he headed for the elevator.

He made no noise as he unlocked the door and slipped into the dim room. Max was sleeping, snoring a little. Jeremiah sat at the desk, watching and waiting for Max to wake up.

2

They left the car in the motel garage and took a cab to the airport, arriving an hour before their flight was scheduled to depart. After picking up the tickets and checking through the overnight bag, the two guns wrapped securely inside, Max and Jeremiah went into the bar.

They hadn't been at the table more than a minute when Jeremiah jumped up again and headed for the men's room, his second such trip since they'd arrived at LaGuardia.

Max watched him go, then shook his head and started to read a copy of the *Times* that someone had left on the table.

Jeremiah finally returned, dropping heavily into the chair and picking up his drink. He finished it quickly and ordered another.

Max folded the paper and set it aside. "You like that can or what?" he said.

"You want to know something?" Jeremiah abruptly asked, downing his whiskey with what seemed to Max a shade too much enthusiasm.

"What?"

"Not only have I never been to Miami before, but I've also never been on an airplane."

Max lowered his drink and eyed him. "Really?"

"Yeah." He smiled a bit shakily. "It sure as hell has been a week of new experiences for me."

Max toasted him. "Well, I'll tell you, kiddo, you've been holding up pretty good."

"You really think so?"

"Sure. Under the circumstances. For you."

Jeremiah seemed pleased with what had to be considered a mixed compliment, at best. He ordered another drink.

"Taking a trip, are you, Max?"

They both stiffened momentarily, until they looked up and saw Aaron Temple and Cody Blaine standing next to the table. Then Max smiled. "We just want some sun."

Blaine nodded. "You do look a little pale, Trueblood. Maybe the pressure is starting to get to you?"

"Pressure?" Max said blandly.

Blaine squeezed into the booth next to Jeremiah and took the last cigarette from a pack. He crumpled the pack. "You guys are hot, we know that. Word is that everybody and his brother are looking for you. Both of you."

"That true?" Jeremiah said. "We hadn't noticed."

Max was amused. Donahue sounded cool. Like he had everything under control. This was apparently the face he chose to show outsiders. Or maybe his courage came from the third drink he was now working on. He lied very well, in any event.

Aaron dragged a chair over and sat down with a sigh. He didn't say anything.

Blaine glanced sidewise at Jeremiah. "God, Aaron, what a couple of gutsy guys they are. The whole fucking Black Hand is looking to eradicate them for good, and here they sit in their pretty Hawaiian shirts waiting to wing off to . . . Miami?"

Jeremiah smiled at him but didn't say anything.

Aaron looked at Max. "You don't look so good."

"Age, Aaron, that's all, just age catching up with me." Max

checked the white-gold Rolex on his wrist. "I hate like hell to break this up when we're all having so much fun, but Donahue and I have a plane to catch."

Jeremiah quickly finished his drink.

Blaine scooted out, then looked down at him. "Actually, you look a little green around the edges, too."

Jeremiah stood. "I'm fine, thank you very much."

Aaron seemed to notice that Max was favoring one side, but he didn't mention it. "Don't get burned," he said instead. "By the sun."

"We'll be careful." Max tossed a bill onto the table.

Jeremiah picked up the briefcase. "Maybe we'll send you a postcard," he said.

They walked toward the concourse.

Jeremiah fastened the seat belt tightly, then gave it one more yank, just to be sure. The whiskey and weariness were beginning to catch up to him. "Lemme tell ya somethin'," he said sloppily, leaning into Max.

"What?"

"I don't like this much. This flying crap."

Max fastened his own seat belt. "We haven't even started to taxi yet."

"Yeah, well. You know, I'd rather be back at the house chasing those two bastards who shot you than doing this."

Max used one hand to push him back into place. "Go to sleep, Jeremiah. We'll be in Miami before you wake up."

And by the time the flight attendant started the usual spiel about flotation devices and emergency exits, Jeremiah was out cold. Max figured that was probably for the best.

He shook a pain pill out of the bottle and waited for the drink cart to appear.

Cody set two cups of coffee onto the table and dropped back into the booth. "You look like a man with something on his mind," he said.

Aaron stopped reading the flight board and grimaced. "Nothing very important, believe me." He reached for the Sweet 'n' Low, then shrugged and took sugar instead. Live a little. "You know what's on my mind, partner? That in three months it's going to be over. For forty years I've followed all the rules and did just what I was supposed to. So what?"

"So maybe they'll give you a gold watch."

"Right. Like I said, Max already has his."

"I noticed. So what are you saying? That crime pays? That you should've been a bad guy?"

"No. No, of course not. But maybe just once I should've done something that didn't come out of the fucking NYPD manual."

"Well, it's not too late."

Aaron stared at him for a moment. "You know what, buddy? You're goddamned right." He smiled. "And do you know what I'm going to do?"

"I have no idea."

"I'm going to catch the next flight to Miami."

Cody put his cup down so hard that some of the coffee inside slopped over onto the table. "Miami? Why the hell?"

He shrugged. "So I can find out how the story ends. Maybe it's as simple as that."

Cody used a paper napkin to clean up the spilled coffee. Then he looked up. "That's a really dumb idea. Guaranteed to get you into some serious hot water."

But Aaron only laughed. "So what the hell are they going to do? Can me?"

"Possibly. Probably."

"Big fucking deal."

"What about me?"

Aaron drank some coffee, then shook his head. "Don't be so self-centered, young man. Not everything in the world revolves around you. This has nothing to do with Cody Blaine."

"You're my partner."

"And so?"

"And so . . ." He drained the cup, then began to break off little pieces of the Styrofoam. "And so that has to mean something, doesn't it?"

"It doesn't mean that you have to shoot yourself in the foot just because I do."

"Maybe it means that."

"Don't play TV hero."

They were quiet briefly, both of them watching the bartender make a whiskey sour. Cody was still crumbling the cup. "We had one of our fights last night, Mandy and me," he said. "She claims that this job is killing my soul. Those were her exact words. Killing my soul."

"Women say things sometimes when they're mad," Aaron said.

"She didn't sound mad when she said it. She didn't sound anything at all. According to her, I don't know how to behave like a real human being anymore. All I know how to do is act like a cop."

Aaron finished his coffee. "Does all of this have a point?"

"I don't know. Maybe not."

"If it matters, Cody, I think your soul is fine. And you're on a fast track within the department. Don't blow it." Aaron stood. "I'll send you a postcard from Miami."

Cody watched him limp away. Crazy old bastard. What the hell was he trying to prove? The question now was, what should a man who wants to prove he still has a soul do next?

"Goddammit," Cody said aloud, startling a nun who was sitting at the next table, almost causing her to spill her 7-Up.

He left the bar and hurried through the concourse, catching up with Aaron at the ticket counter. "You think you're pretty fucking smart, don't you?"

Aaron glanced at him. "What on earth are you babbling about?"

"Thought you'd put one over on me, didn't you? Aaron Temple, renegade cop, going off to Miami alone and maybe busting a few big ones. Comes back a hero. And his partner who stayed home playing with himself looks like the dope of the year. Right? Well, no way, partner. Whither thou goest."

Aaron shook his head. "You're crazy."

"Maybe. But maybe I'm just being smart like you. If something good does come down, I want to be close enough for some of the glory to rub off on me."

"And what if it goes bad? You want the shit rubbing off on you too?"

Cody took out his credit card. "I'll take my chances, partner."

Aaron gave up. "Fine," he said. "Come if you want. But don't say I didn't warn you."

Cody just smiled and stepped to the counter.

three:

it's not how you play the game

1

Jeremiah woke up when the sun, pouring in through the window of their beachfront hotel room, reached his bed. He blinked twice, trying to orient himself, then sat up.

Max was across the large room, out of bed, but not doing anything except sitting on the couch, staring out the window. He didn't seem to notice that Jeremiah was awake and watching him.

After a minute Jeremiah swung his feet to the floor. "Life sure can get fucked up fast, can't it?" he said.

Max glanced at him. "Okay," he said. "I give up. Is that a philosophical statement or the answer to a puzzle?"

"I don't know. Mostly it was just me talking. Maybe I feel a little guilty. I mean, this is sort of my fault. You had that great loft and everything was going fine, but now . . . well, you know what I mean."

"That's a bigger load of crap than usual—even for you, Donahue." Max stood and walked over to the window, peering downward. "First of all, everybody is responsible for his own life. You didn't pull the fucking wool over my eyes. I knew from the beginning what you were and what was going on. No matter what you might like to think about your own clever mind, I was the one who orchestrated this whole fuck-up, not you." He turned to face Jeremiah. "Remember that."

"Yes, sir," Jeremiah said.

"And second of all, you're forgetting one very important thing."

"What's that?"

"Just that if you hadn't walked into this situation grinning and playing everybody's best buddy, Tadzio would have hired somebody else to do the job. That somebody else probably wouldn't have had your . . . sensitivity. He would have blown me away quite cheerfully."

"Or he would have tried, anyway," Jeremiah said with a slight smile.

"He would have tried, yes. So, if you want to get really ridiculous about it, we could even say you saved my life."

"Shit," Jeremiah said.

"Uh-huh."

Something about the notion of himself as the hero of this mess made Jeremiah uncomfortable. He stood and headed for the bathroom. "I'm going to take a shower," he said.

He stayed in the fancy bathroom a long time, using the coconut-scented shampoo provided by the hotel and calling the time on the phone by the tub, just for the hell of it.

Finally, he emerged and began to dress, putting on the second pair of new jeans and the other shirt, which was purple and yellow and his favorite. Max took the other clothes from the bag. "Call room service," he said. "Order up some breakfast."

"What should I get?"

"Whatever." He closed the bathroom door, and the shower started again.

After a careful study of the menu Jeremiah took Max at his word. He ordered steak and eggs for two, hash browns, OJ, toast, and coffee. While he waited for the meal he sat on the windowsill and watched the people on the beach below. They all seemed to be enjoying themselves. Even though it was still fairly early, the pool below was already jammed. Everybody seemed to be enjoying themselves.

Must be nice, he thought.

It was a little weird that here he was, living better than he ever had, in terms of things like this fancy hotel, and yet he wasn't happy. Of course, people wanted to kill him, so that would tend to take the edge off a good time.

Weirder still: He wasn't really unhappy, either. He didn't know what the hell he was feeling. Except hungry. Where the heck was room service?

Max was out and dressed, and they were watching some news on the television by the time the food finally arrived. When the tray was safely deposited and the waiter gone, Jeremiah started uncovering the plates. Max looked bemused. "You hungry or what?"

"Well, I think that an opportunity like this should be grabbed. I mean, you never know when the chance to eat will come along again."

"Probably not until lunch, at least."

"Maybe," Jeremiah said ominously.

After a moment Max nodded. "You have a point. Well, if necessary, this could keep us for a week." Max still looked a little pale, and Jeremiah noticed that he touched his bandaged side occasionally during the meal.

"Maybe you should see a doctor down here," he suggested tentatively. "Just to follow up."

But Max shook his head.

Before Jeremiah could pursue the question, or even decide if he should pursue it, the phone rang, startling him. "Who the hell knows where we're at?" he asked.

"Probably everybody on the whole goddamned East Coast," Max said, going to answer it.

Jeremiah decided not to listen to the one-sided conversation. It would probably just upset him. Instead, he concentrated on finishing his food. He was just swallowing the last bite when Max came back to the table. "Well?"

"We're going over later to a café called the Blue Parrot. In Little Havana."

"I can hardly wait."

"It seems that certain people are interested in talking to me about the book."

"I'm sure."

Max sat down again and took a final swallow of coffee. "The voice on the phone said that maybe a deal can be made."

Jeremiah shoved away the empty plate. "And what does the great Max Trueblood say?"

"Nothing much at this point."

"You won't give them the book, will you, Max?"

Max wiped his mouth carefully with the snowy linen napkin. "No. Of course not. What the book is, mostly, is a bargaining chip. As long as they think I might be persuaded to give it up, we'll be okay. But the ledger stays right in the hotel safe for the time being."

"Will that work? Really?"

Max gave him a dirty look. "All of a sudden you want a written guarantee?"

"No. I was just expressing a healthy curiosity."

"Maybe not so healthy as all that." Max glanced at Jeremiah's shirt. "At least you're dressed for Little Havana."

"Ha, ha." Jeremiah went over to the closet and reached into the pocket of his Windbreaker. "You want this?" he asked. "It's real silk." He held out the wrinkled tie.

Max took it and held it up against the white shirt. "Just what I needed," he said somewhat doubtfully. "Thanks."

Jeremiah shrugged. He picked up the tray of dirty dishes and set it outside the door.

Carefully balancing two cups of vending machine coffee, Cody Blaine kicked at the door of room 147 in the Sand Dunes Motel. There were no sand dunes anywhere in the general vicinity, but he supposed the name of the place fell under what they called poetic licence. What the old Sand Dunes did have were rooms that cost only twenty-five dollars a night. He kicked again, more forcefully.

Finally, Aaron opened the door.

"Christ, I thought you died or something in here," Cody complained.

"Or something." Aaron took one of the cups from him and sipped the coffee. He looked dismayed. "Hell, this tastes like battery acid."

"Hey, if you want your quarter back, fine."

Aaron shook his head. "No, that's all right. You did your best."

Cody snorted and sat down on one of the narrow beds.

"Actually," Aaron said, sitting as well, "I was on the telephone."

"To New York?"

"No. After thinking about it I decided that call was a pleasure that could wait awhile."

"Great. You think they'll can us?"

Aaron lowered his cup and frowned at him. "Hey, sweetheart, you knew the risks when you signed on for this little adventure. If you're going to start bitching about it, I'd just as soon you caught the next commuter flight back."

"Ease up. I wasn't saying anything like that. I was just wondering."

"Okay," Aaron said.

"So who were you talking to?"

"Friend of mine named Luke Sinclair. He was a cop in the city for years, then came down here to work. Retired a while back, but he still has some connections. I wanted to see if maybe he could help us track down Trueblood and Donahue."

"And did he have any idea where our wandering boys might be?"

"He'll get back to me. Or I'll get back to him."

"And in the meantime?"

"Well, I don't know. Maybe we'll just sit here and wait. Or we could hit the streets and see what turns up."

"I'd rather do that," Cody said. "But we don't know these streets. That might be a problem."

"Streets is streets," Aaron said succinctly. "Besides, half the creeps down here are New Yorkers on vacation. We should be able to turn over some familiar rocks."

"Suits me," Cody said. "At least that way we'll get to see some of the city. Why waste the trip?"

Aaron finished his coffee and tossed the cup into the wastebasket. "Oh, I don't think this trip is going to be wasted," he said.

"You don't?"

"Hell, no." Aaron gave one of his rare smiles. "I think we're going to have a hell of a good time. Come on, let's go rent a car."

Cody gulped down the last of the terrible coffee and quickly followed him from the room.

2

Jeremiah sat in the Hertz car in the parking lot while Max went into the department store to buy himself a sport jacket. It was mostly so he could wear his shoulder holster, Max had said, but he also knew that he wanted to feel a little better dressed. He found a nice job in linen that fit fine right off the rack, then paused to look at the ties. But in the end he just paid for the jacket and smoothed a few more of the wrinkles out of the tie he was wearing.

In about twenty minutes he was back in the car. He donned the holster and then the jacket. "Now I'm ready for the Blue Parrot," he said.

Jeremiah took the other gun and shoved it into the waistband of his jeans, letting the long tail of his shirt cover it.

"This is just a meet we're going to, right?" he said. "Just to talk, isn't that what you said?"

"Life is full of surprises, kiddo. Best to be prepared."

They drove to Calle Ocho, the main drag of the area known as Little Havana where the first Cuban refugees had settled some twenty-odd years earlier. It was like being in a foreign country. All the signs were in Spanish, as was the conversation they could hear outside the car windows. Small groups of Cubans were gathered around the espresso stands, just as they had done back in their former country.

"I was in Havana once," Max said suddenly.

"Yeah?" Jeremiah seemed surprised at the personal revelation. He glanced at Max as he turned off Calle Ocho and onto a side street.

"Years ago."

"Working?"

Max shrugged, then he said, "Yeah. Hit a guy who was selling guns to the wrong side in the revolution."

"Which side was that?"

"Don't know," Max said. "I never asked."

Jeremiah laughed softly.

"There's the place," Max said suddenly. "Stop here."

Jeremiah stopped and turned off the engine, then looked around. "Where?"

"There. Blue Parrot."

He looked blankly at the Spanish words. "Okay, if you say so."

The Blue Parrot didn't look like a hot tourist stop, although the food was probably authentic and maybe even good. Probably the locals hung out here, the same kind of locals who patronized shabby little places like this back in the city.

The inside didn't improve the image.

Even though the lunch hour should have been at its peak by the time they walked in, there wasn't a customer in the place. "They're not exactly doing a landslide business, are they?" Jeremiah said.

"Maybe the spics know something about the place that we don't," Max replied as they crossed the room and chose a corner table. He sat with his back to the wall, giving himself a clear view of the door.

"Maybe I won't order a taco, after all."

"You don't order a taco in a Cuban joint, stupid," Max said absently. "You order white bean soup and arroz con pollo."

"Uh-huh, sure I do."

"That's chicken with rice."

"Well, I'll remember that the next time we're in Cuba. But right now I don't seem to have much of an appetite."

"I know what you mean."

There was one man in the café, and he looked like maybe he was a waiter, but he made no move at all in their direction. Instead, he stayed where he was, on the other side of the room. He was very busy folding napkins.

Jeremiah stirred in the chair. "This feels strange to me," he said. "I'm not the expert, Max, but maybe this wasn't such a good idea coming here like this."

"You might be right for a change," Max said. He put his hand inside the jacket and touched the gun. Maybe he had read this whole thing wrong.

Before they could discuss it any further, or decide what might be the best move to make now, the door opened and five men filed in. Maybe they were the lunch bunch. But they didn't pick a table. One of them had an overcoat draped over his arm. When all five were standing around Max and Jeremiah, he let the coat slip to the floor. He was holding a Uzi.

Great neighborhood, Max thought. And people talked about New York.

One of the men stepped forward. "Hello, Max," he said.

Max recognized him, though not with any sense of pleasure. "Well, Buster, it's been years, hasn't it? You've put on weight," he said pleasantly. "And learned to speak. Congratulations." Regretfully, he took his hand from the gun.

"You always was a real funny guy, Max," Buster said.

Max glanced at the others, recognizing all but one of the men. He might have been a local; he had a great tan. "Tadzio sent you down here to flatter me, right?"

"Wrong, asshole."

"I thought this was going to be a negotiating session. Shouldn't they have sent someone with the ability to think?"

"We're smart enough to do what's supposed to be done, don't you worry about that." Buster gave a signal with his head, and the man with the Uzi stepped forward, poking the barrel of the gun into Jeremiah's neck. "You're coming with us," Buster said.

"Is that really necessary?" Jeremiah said. "I haven't even tried the arroz can pollo yet."

The gun poked harder.

"Okay, okay, I had big breakfast, anyway."

Max sighed, not really surprised but angry at himself for not being ready for this. It seemed more and more as if the gray cells were not working quite like they used to. "Raphael will be in touch, I guess," he said.

"That's up to Mr. Tadzio."

"Of course it is. Well, could you give him a message for me?"

"Yeah. What?"

Max turned his gaze to Jeremiah for a moment, then back to Buster. "Make sure he understands one thing. I will not negotiate for damaged goods."

Jeremiah made an effort that showed and smiled; it was shaky but it worked. "That should make me feel better, right?"

Max gave him a thumbs-up gesture, then looked at Buster once again. "Make sure he knows that, Buster."

"Yeah, yeah, big fucking deal. Come on, asshole."

Jeremiah got to his feet. The coat was picked up and draped over the Uzi again, but the barrel was pointed right at him. One of the men reached under Jeremiah's shirt and took out the gun, then all six of them walked out. The café got very quiet.

Max stayed where he was for a little bit, thinking. Then he glanced over at the man folding the napkins. "No wonder you don't do a better business in here," he said. "Something like that sort of takes the edge right off the appetite."

As he drove the rented car back to their fancy hotel Max realized, with no little dismay, that it was altogether too easy to become accustomed to the company of another person. This was the first time in what seemed like days that he had actually been alone. After a lifetime of solitude he certainly should have been accustomed to the feeling, but it occurred to him during the drive that there must be some subtle difference between being alone and being lonely. It was a difference that had escaped him for sixty-five fairly contented years, but one that he was now aware of. The awareness did not please him.

Well, you had to give him credit: When Max Trueblood fucked up his life, he did a first-class job of it.

He left the car for the valet to park and went into the hotel. As he was crossing the lobby he saw Aaron Temple and that partner of his standing by the elevators. He hesitated, then kept going until he reached them.

"Down for the sun?" he asked.

They both turned and saw him. "Maybe," Aaron said. "Or the show."

"Well, have a good time." He pressed the up button and pretended to watch the lights marking the rapid descent of the elevator.

Blaine seemed to be racing to finish his cigarette before the arrival of the car. "Aren't you missing something?" he asked, exhaling hugely.

"What's that?"

"Your faithful shadow. Tonto. Pancho. Robin. Or Kato. Whoever the hell he is."

Max watched the lights again, until the elevator arrived and the doors slid open. Then he glanced at Aaron. "Well, if you aren't doing anything," he said, "you might as well come up."

Blaine dropped the last of the cigarette into a sand-filled stone urn, and they got onto the elevator. Although they were alone, no one spoke during the ride.

Max unlocked the door and led the way into the room. Still without a word, he went to the small bar in the corner and poured three whiskies.

"None for me," Blaine said.

Max just shrugged. He drained one glass where he stood, then carried the other two across the room and handed one to Aaron. They all sat. "What happened is, they snatched Donahue," he said finally. "Couple of Tadzio's boys."

"Well, that's not really unexpected, is it?" Aaron said.

"I guess not. Of course not. I should have fucking expected it. But it just never occurred to me." Max sipped his drink. "Couple of Marberg's boys were there too."

"That makes sense. Everybody is hot for you now. We told you that."

"Yeah, yeah. You told us." Max slumped back against the couch. "You know about the book, I guess."

"Everybody knows about the fucking book. You didn't exactly keep it a secret, right?"

"Right." Max twisted the glass around in his fingers thoughtfully. "I just thought that was the best way to handle it."

"Probably it was," Aaron said.

"Of course, if we could ask Donahue right now, he might not feel that way," Blaine put in.

Max looked at him, then at Aaron. "You want to tell your partner to keep his goddamned opinions to himself?"

"I think we should all just keep our cool," Aaron said. He set his drink aside. "You know that the minute any one of them gets a hold of the book, you immediately become very, very expendable."

"Of course."

"So?"

Max drank. "So?" he said then. "What am I supposed to say to that? So . . . nothing."

Nobody said anything. The phone rang. Max leaned across the back of the couch to answer it. "Yes?"

He didn't recognize the voice, but that didn't matter. "There's only one way this is going down," the man said. "The book for Donahue. You got one chance to make the switch."

"Yeah, yeah, save the Cagney impression for somebody who gives a shit. Where and when?" He held out a hand, and Aaron gave him a pen and notepad. He wrote quickly, listening. "That's where."

"When is nine o'clock tonight. Be there or Donahue buys it."

"Don't make threats to me," Max said in an icy voice. "You just tell Tadzio or Marberg or whoever is behind this one thing. Donahue better be there, and he better be healthy."

"You just worry about your end of the deal." The man hung up.

Max listened to the dial tone for a moment, then replaced the receiver. "This just gets better and better," he said wearily.

"Beats the hell out of *Miami Vice*," Aaron said. "I think maybe we'll just tag along on this little get-together."

Max looked at him in mild amazement. "Cops? I don't think so."

"Just us two. Who knows, we might come in handy."

"I'm sure." Max walked over to the bar and poured himself another drink. His side was aching, and he swallowed another pain pill as well. "Is that the new policy of the New York cops? Helping the bad guys?"

"The department doesn't even know we're here," Blaine said. He didn't sound or look real thrilled by the whole thing.

"Great. A couple of mavericks. Just what I need. Well, thanks, but no thanks. I can handle this."

"Can you?" Aaron shrugged. "Okay, man. You must know your business. But I was just assuming that you wanted to get away with both Donahue and the book safe."

"I do."

"Then maybe you want to reconsider."

Max hesitated, massaging his side carefully. "No strings?"

"Strings? What the hell kind of strings could a couple of hotdogging mavericks be holding?"

"What's your game, Temple?"

Aaron looked disgusted. "Max, do you want us there or not? We could go fucking sight-seeing, you know. Maybe get a tan."

Finally, Max nodded.

"Terrific," Blaine muttered.

Aaron studied the selection of cigars in the hotel smoke shop.

"So just what am I supposed to do?" Cody asked again, impatiently.

"Go to the cops. Tell them what's coming down. Within limits."

"Within limits. You keep saying that. What the hell does it mean?"

Aaron picked up two of the good stogies and paid for them. "Be discreet, for chrissake," he said as they walked back out into the lobby. Max was standing by the main entrance of the hotel, waiting. "You worked Vice, you must've learned how to be discreet."

"I think what you're really saying is not to get Trueblood and Donahue into hot water with the Miami cops."

Aaron smiled. "Pretty much."

"I don't understand."

Aaron tapped him on the chest with one of the cigars. "So maybe I don't, either, really. But isn't it fun?"

Cody just shook his head and walked away.

Aaron joined Max. "Ready to walk on the beach?"

Max stopped rubbing his side. "I guess. Where's Junior going?"

Aaron shrugged. "He gets itchy. He'll be back."

They walked for five minutes before either man spoke again. It was Max who broke the silence. "Somewhere along the line," he said, "I lost control of this whole thing."

"Yeah," Aaron agreed. "It sure as hell isn't the typical Trueblood operation. You were always flawless. This thing . . . boy, it's full of holes."

"You're telling me." He watched the swimmers. "What a joke. Tadzio hired Donahue, you know. To off me after—"

He stopped.

"After? Hypothetically speaking, the Costa hit?"

Max nodded. "Hypothetically."

"But?"

"But he didn't do the job. If he had, he'd be sitting pretty right now."

"You think so?"

"Yeah." Max seemed to turn that over in his mind briefly, then he said, "Well, maybe. Maybe he was being set up too. Scapegoat time. That would explain a lot."

"Such as?"

"Such as why they gave a job like that to a novice like him in the first place. That never did make sense to me."

Aaron didn't say anything.

"I should have pulled the plug on this thing right at the beginning."

"So why didn't you?"

"Why didn't I? Good question. Let me ask you one. How come a man throws up forty years as a cop and comes running to Miami on some kind of wild-goose chase?"

"Is that what I'm doing? Chasing wild geese?"

"I don't know what the hell you're chasing, Aaron."

"Don't you."

Max stared at the sand for a long time, then he looked up. "Sure I do. You're chasing the same thing I am. Maybe one

more chance to do something. One more chance to . . . feel
something, excitement maybe, before they stick us in a hole
someplace and forget we ever existed."

Aaron only shrugged.

Max shook his head. "Christ, they should have shipped the
both of us off to a home a long time ago. Come on, let's go
back. I'm thirsty."

They turned and started back for the hotel.

four:

only when i laugh

1

The turkey named Buster kept the television playing all the time. Jeremiah listened to the soaps and cartoons this bunch seemed to favor, but he couldn't see the screen because of the way he was tied to the bed in the run-down motel room.

He tried to wriggle his hands and feet every once in a while, just so the blood would keep flowing. If the chance came to make a break, he didn't want to be falling all over himself.

The chance never came, though.

At some point during the day Raphael Tadzio came into the room. Everybody else scurried out. Tadzio and good old Ichabod Crane stood next to the bed, looking down at him. He felt like a bug pinned to a board.

He smiled. "Hard as hell to get good help these days, right, Mr. Tadzio?"

The skinny man in the black suit hit him across the face.

Tadzio crossed his arms. "I don't need to hear any of your lip, Donahue. I just wanted to see you one more time."

"Sentimental fool."

That earned him another slap.

He was beginning not to like Ichabod very much.

Tadzio shook his head and left the room, followed by the slapper. In a minute the others came back, and the television went on again.

Jeremiah listened for a while, then he raised his head a little. "You know," he said, "I'd really like to use the john. If nobody minds."

After a muttered consultation with the other stooges Buster untied him and they walked across the room. Buster, thank goodness, stopped at the door. "I'll be right here," he warned. "So don't try nothing funny."

Jeremiah looked at him. "Buster, I haven't done anything funny in the can since I was fourteen."

When the door closed, he unzipped his jeans and took a thoughtful leak. The one-sided phone conversation with Max had told him enough to know what was going on. A big swap was supposed to come down, him for the book. Fat chance of that happening, even if these fools thought so. Max had his faults, but as far as he had seen, pure stupidity wasn't among them. There was no way that he would give up his insurance policy.

And Jeremiah didn't blame him for a minute.

He finished and washed his hands carefully. A man didn't want to go to his eternal reward with dirty fingers.

When he had stalled for about as long as he thought wise, Jeremiah checked his fly and opened the door. True to his word, Buster was still poised on the threshold. "All yours," Jeremiah said.

It was long after dark by the time they untied him again. Everybody marched out to the car and climbed in. Sitting between Buster, who sweated a lot, and a skinny kid who smelled of too much Old Spice, Jeremiah tried not to breathe too deeply. His hands were still tightly bound behind his back.

After a forty-minute drive they parked on an empty strip of

beach. It was almost as bright as day because of the full moon overhead.

"Is this where we're meeting Max?" Jeremiah asked.

Nobody bothered to answer him. Another car pulled up beside them. Tadzio and Crane were inside, along with two men he didn't know at all. They looked important, even from here. Everybody sure did want that book. And it seemed to him that not only would these guys want to keep the cops from getting it, but also any of their rivals.

Boyohboy, Donahue, when you step in it, you do it fine.

It was almost fifteen minutes before he saw the headlights of another car approaching. Jeremiah recognized the rented Ford. So what was the old bastard up to? Jeremiah hadn't really expected him to show up at all. The Ford parked a couple hundred feet from them and Max got out.

Shit, Jeremiah thought, *tell me he's not going to do this. I cannot fucking believe it*.

They all unloaded from the backseat and he took a deep swallow of clean air. "Signal him that you're okay," Buster ordered.

Jeremiah looked at him. "With what, dummy?"

Somebody used a very sharp knife on the rope, and he was free. He raised one hand in a half wave.

Max responded by holding up a black ledger.

"You start walking," Buster said. "Slow. And you stop when I tell you to."

"Sure thing."

"Okay, go."

"It's been fun, boys," Jeremiah said. "Let's do it again sometime." He took one careful step, followed by several others. Max was watching him closely, and although he couldn't see them, he could feel the guns at his back. When he had covered about half the distance to where Max was, Buster yelled at him to stop.

He stopped.

"Throw the book," Buster yelled.

The ledger came flying through the air and landed very near his feet.

"Take three steps away."

He was getting very tired of Buster's voice. "Mother, may I?" he muttered, then he did.

Behind him there was the sound of footsteps on the wet sand, and he was just thinking that maybe this was going to go down just the way the bad guys wanted it to when suddenly all hell broke loose.

"*Freeze!*" The shout came from some place in the dunes.

Jeremiah looked around, bewildered.

Then the first shot rang out. Its echo seemed to hang in the night air for one long moment, then it was drowned by a barrage of gunfire that came from everywhere.

Even above all the noise Jeremiah could hear Max yelling at him to get his ass in gear and move. He started for the car, then suddenly he whirled around and ran back to where Buster was picking up the book. He kicked Buster in the balls, then again, in the face. Buster hit the sand with a thud, letting go of the book, and Jeremiah swept it up.

Max was still yelling at him.

Now he ran full-speed toward the car. Max had the door open, and as Jeremiah reached him, he grabbed him by one arm and threw him across the seat.

Max shoved himself behind the wheel and leaned on the horn, like he was signaling somebody. Jeremiah peeked over the dash and saw Cody Blaine—what the hell was he doing here, anyway?—run by with a lot of other cops.

Max shoved the car into drive and they took off.

Jeremiah tried to right himself in the seat. "Max," he said.

"Stay down and shut up," Max said tightly.

Jeremiah obeyed.

Cody saw Aaron come out from behind a dune, and he stopped to wait for him. The Miami cops kept going, still exchanging gunfire with the startled bad guys.

"They made it away clean, with the book," Cody said, gulping in some air. Shit, his lungs were shot to hell.

Aaron nodded. "Come on, then, let's see this thing through."

They started after the other cops.

Later Cody always thought that he had heard the very bullet that had hit Aaron, although logically he knew that was impossible. It was in the final blast of gunfire before the end. Aaron stumbled, seemed to recover his balance, then dropped heavily.

Cody knelt beside him in the sand. "Hey, Aaron," he said. "Aaron?"

"S'okay," Aaron said.

But it was far from okay, and Cody knew that when he saw the gaping hole in Aaron's chest. He put a hand over it and pressed, trying to stanch the gushing blood. It was quiet all around them now; even the sound of the surf was drowned out by the raspy sound of Aaron's lungs trying to work. Somebody bent down to say that an ambulance was on its way. Cody leaned closer to Aaron. "Hang in there, partner," he whispered. "Hang in there."

Aaron tried to say something, but the words were too soft to hear.

"It's not fair," Cody said to nobody. "Damn, this isn't fair."

He was still bent there, holding his hand over the wound, when the medics finally arrived, shoving him out of the way. He stepped back, knowing it was too late. The men in white went to work quickly and efficiently.

Cody looked away from their efforts and saw a Miami detective approach. The man was wearing a sky-blue suit and dark glasses, despite the fact that it was night. He did not look happy. "You want to tell me the whole story of what was going on here?" the man said.

"In a minute," Cody replied. He waited until the medics conceded what he had already known. They sat back, starting to put their equipment away. "Damn," Cody said. "Damn."

"Who's the old guy?"

Cody stared at the dark glasses. "That's my partner," he said. "Aaron Temple. Best damned cop I ever saw."

"So how come a New York cop is dead on my beach here? You want to tell me that?"

"It wasn't supposed to happen like this," Cody said. "Aaron only wanted to find out how the story ended."

"Well, it's ended for him. You're not telling me anything, Blaine. You come into my office and say maybe something is going to happen down here, maybe I could bust some biggies if I show up with a few men. And so, fucking World War Three breaks out. I got two guys hurt, one dead creep, three in custody, and one dead Yankee cop. I want to know what the hell just happened here."

Cody stayed quiet as he watched the medics leave, then he shivered a little and took a deep breath. He started talking in a low voice, giving the angry cop a heavily edited version of the night's events. He did what Aaron had wanted and kept Trueblood and Donahue out of it.

2

There didn't seem to be any need for conversation until they were back in the hotel room. Once inside, Jeremiah, who had been clutching the ledger to his chest like some kind of shield against God knew what, held it out. "Here," he said.

Max took it and thumbed the pages idly. "Thank you."

"Were you really going to let them have it?"

"No. I would've gotten it back. Maybe I would've run Buster over. But you took care of it for me. So thanks."

"I owed you."

Max went to the bar and poured two drinks. He brought them back and sat on the couch with Jeremiah. "Nobody owes anybody anything," he said. "We do what we do because we want to."

Jeremiah shook his head slightly, then said, "Okay. In that case, thanks for wanting to spring me from those creeps."

"You're welcome."

"I guess we're still in deep shit, though, huh?"

"Oh, yes." Max didn't seem terribly concerned about any of it.

Jeremiah wanted to ask him what they should do next, but he figured that Max wouldn't answer him and might get mad, so he didn't say anything.

They were still drinking and thinking about the shit they were in when there was a knock at the door. Jeremiah put down his glass, picked up Max's gun, and went to answer it.

Cody Blaine brushed past him into the room and spoke to Max. "I came to tell you that Aaron is dead," he said flatly. "One of those bastards offed him."

Jeremiah sank back down onto the couch. "Christ," he said.

Max shook his head. "I'm sorry about that."

"Yeah," Cody said. "Me too. I'm sorry, too."

"Aaron should have stayed in New York. He understood things in the city."

Cody smiled a little and shrugged. There was dried blood on his hands, but he didn't seem to know it. Or care, anyway, if he did know. "He wanted to find out what was going to happen here. And he didn't want to live in Westchester."

"What?"

"Never mind, Max, it doesn't matter." Cody seemed to notice the blood suddenly, and he wiped his hands uselessly on the front of his jeans. "I did what Aaron asked and covered for you with the locals. But you probably want to get out of town. Go someplace quiet. Maybe Alaska."

Max was looking at him curiously. "And what about you?"

"I'm going home. Fight to stay a cop if I have to. There are some people I want to get. Like Tadzio. He got away tonight. I'm going to get the bastards. Get them and shut them down."

Max smiled faintly. "Now you sound like your partner."

Cody seemed to think about that. "Guess I'm stuck with it,"

he said. "I'm going now. But I wanted to tell you about Aaron myself."

He turned and left the room.

Max got up. "You wait here," he said.

"Where are you going?"

"Nowhere." He sighed. "Just downstairs for a minute."

"Be careful."

He caught up with Cody, still waiting for the elevator, and rode down with him in silence. When they reached the lobby, Max led the way to a corner love seat that was shrouded by potted palms. They both sat, and Blaine lighted a cigarette.

"It's your dime," he said finally.

"I want you to have the book," Max said.

"The book? Your fucking book?"

"Yes."

Blaine's eyes narrowed. "But that's the only thing that might—might—keep you alive."

"Well, I know that," Max said. "And I didn't mean I'm giving you the book right now. But when I . . . don't need it anymore, it'll be coming to you."

"When you're dead," Cody said.

"Yes." How easily the young could talk about death, even now, when the image of Aaron's dying still burned in his eyes. "There's enough information in there to give you a career. Bust the ones you can and make a name for yourself."

"Fine. Whatever. Your book for my partner. Not exactly what I'd call a fair trade, but I'm not stupid enough to turn you down."

"Good. There is one thing."

"Of course. There always is. What?"

Max watched a very fat woman cross the lobby with a very small dog clutched to her ample chest. "If Donahue is still around, you know, if he doesn't check out with me, I want you to use the book or whatever else it takes to keep him alive if you can." He turned his head and looked at Cody. "Understand?"

"I understand. But it's not what I would have expected. Nobility from Max Trueblood?"

"There's nothing noble about it," Max said impatiently. "It's just something I want. Okay? Do we have a deal?"

Cody held out his bloodstained hand and they shook. "We have a deal, Max."

Max sat on the love seat and watched Blaine cross the lobby and leave the hotel.

When Max got back upstairs, he found that Jeremiah had changed into a pair of blue-and-green-striped swimming trunks. "What the hell is this? You've decided that we're on vacation all of a sudden?"

Jeremiah shrugged. "Why the hell not? Might as well have some fun. Come on."

"What do you mean, 'come on'? I don't swim, even when I'm not taped up like a goddamned mummy."

"You don't have to swim, Mummy. Just come down to the fucking pool with me. What should we do, sit here and grow old together?"

"I'm already old."

"And I'm getting there fast, so there's no time to waste." Jeremiah draped a towel around his neck. "Come on. I just want to do a few laps, then we can come back up here and talk all the serious shit you want."

Max didn't have the energy to argue anymore. It was easier just to go. He tucked his gun back into the holster and took the whiskey bottle and a glass with him.

It was too late for swimming, of course, so no one else was in the pool. They stepped over the chain. Max sat in a chaise lounge and poured himself a drink.

Jeremiah did a few slow laps, then hoisted himself out of the pool, standing precariously on the edge. "Hey, Max."

"Hmm?"

"So what are our chances? You think the bastards are going to get us?"

Max was watching the play of the lights across the surface of the pool. "Probably. Eventually."

Jeremiah shook water from his hair like a wet dog. "Well, we won't make it easy for them."

"Hell, no," Max said absently. "We'll make the motherfuckers sweat."

Jeremiah smiled.

Max tried to concentrate on his drink and his thoughts. "Max?"

"What?" he said sharply.

"Tomorrow?"

"Maybe. How do I fucking know?" He looked up again, impatiently. "Thought you wanted to swim?"

"Yeah, okay."

Jeremiah stood where he was for a moment, then he made a sound that was vaguely reminiscent of that made by a machine gun. He clutched his stomach and groaned. "They got me," he said. "The sons of bitches got me."

With one more groan he fell backward into the water like a stone, splashing everything within reach, including the chaise lounge.

Max laughed.